This book belongs to

. . . .

CONTENTS

Edited by Chloe Boyes. *Designed by* Pritty Ramjee.
Cover illustrated by Stuart Trotter.
Endpapers illustrated by John Harrold.

THE
RUPERT®
ANNUAL

EXPRESS NEWSPAPERS

EGMONT
We bring stories to life

Published in Great Britain 2018 by Egmont UK Limited
The Yellow Building, 1 Nicholas Road, London W11 4AN
Rupert Bear™ & © Express Newspapers & DreamWorks Distribution Limited.
All Rights Reserved.

ISBN 978 1 4052 9119 4
68611/001
Printed in Italy

No. 83

RUPERT and the

SUGAR BIRD

" A story of how
a kind action by
Rupert to a little
bird saves him
from trouble."

RUPERT MEETS A STRANGER

While Rupert reads a story book,
His mother cries, "Come here and look,"

A pink-white bird has perched nearby;
To see it closer he will try.

It's quickly out of sight again,
And Rupert's chase has been in vain.

He sees the brothers Fox, but they
Turn round and run the other way.

One day Rupert has nothing to do, so he takes a book and begins to read. He has not read far when he is interrupted by Mrs Bear. "Come and look here, Rupert," she says in a strange voice. He quickly joins her at the window, and, gazing out, he sees a plump pink-and-white bird sitting on a branch. "What an odd-looking creature," says the little bear. "It might almost be made of sugar."

Hurriedly putting on his scarf Rupert goes out, only to find that the queer bird has disappeared. "It's no good," he sighs, "nobody can run as fast as a bird flying; I'd better go home again." On regaining the lane he sees the two brothers, Freddy and Ferdy Fox, ahead of him. To his surprise, the Foxes turn and run the other way.

The Foxes have quite disappeared;
Says Rupert, "Everything's most weird."

Then birds he sees, all chattering round
An object lying on the ground.

He hurries quickly to the spot:
A sugar Easter egg they've got.

"Who can have brought it?" croaks a crow,
"That's what we birds all want to know."

On reaching the place where the Foxes were, Rupert finds that they, too, have disappeared. Further on he pauses by a fence and peeps through. A lot of sparrows and thrushes and crows are hovering round a certain spot in the field and are chattering loudly. "There must be something interesting in the grass," thinks the little bear. "I'd like to go and see what it is. Surely they wouldn't fly away from me too."

Climbing the fence, Rupert reaches the place where the birds are settling round a smooth round object in the grass. He picks it up and finds it very heavy. "Why, it's a huge Easter egg," he gasps, "and made of sugar. What on earth is it doing here?" "That's just what we'd like to know," croaks an old crow, "the real question is—who brought it? It's a very serious matter."

RUPERT SHOWS THE EGG

The sugar bird again appears,
Flies up to Rupert, "Thief!" he jeers;

His mother says, "It puzzles me;
Ask Mrs Sheep what it can be."

Says Mrs Sheep, "No eggs are here,
It's early for them yet, my dear."

Then Rupert sees the Wise Old Goat
Who on a problem new will dote.

Rupert is impressed by what the crow has said and runs home to ask his mother. On the way the queer bird he had been chasing suddenly appears and flies straight for him. "Thief! Thief! Thief!" screeches the bird. At home, Mrs Bear also is very puzzled by the egg. "It may have been taken from the sweet shop," she suggests. "I should trot along and ask old Mrs Sheep if she has missed it."

Hastening to the sweet shop Rupert shows the egg. Mrs Sheep looks at him in astonishment. "It hasn't been stolen from here," she says. Rupert, more mystified than ever, starts homewards. While crossing a field he sees the familiar figure of the Wise Old Goat. "He's just the man. He loves solving mysteries," thinks the little bear. "I'll ask him."

RUPERT GETS ADVICE

The Goat hears Rupert's tale all through,
Then says, "Here's my advice to you:

Replace the egg upon the ground
Exactly where it first was found."

He hasn't gone so very far,
When angry birds cry, "There you are."

One takes the egg, and others say,
"Explain! How came that egg your way."

The Wise Old Goat is very surprised at seeing the egg and listens carefully to what Rupert tells him. "There's something suspicious about this," he says gravely. "Nobody ought to have Easter eggs as early as this. My advice to you is—put it back exactly where you found it." Rupert thanks him and moves rather sadly away. "It seems a pity," he thinks; "it's such a lovely egg."

Rupert has no chance of carrying out his intention. At the sound of heavy wings he turns and finds several large birds swooping towards him. One of them seizes the egg from his hands and flies off with it. "Why, I believe you are all made of sugar!" he gasps. "Never mind that," says a bird sternly. "The point is: a lot of eggs have been stolen and we find you holding one of them. How do you explain that?"

"We don't believe you," cries a bird;
"Show us the field where this occurred."

They reach the spot, up flies a crow,
Who says, "He's not a thief, I know."

"Someone's a thief," the birds declare;
"We mean to hunt him everywhere."

Then Rupert finds, exhausted, weak,
The bird he'd earlier gone to seek.

Rupert insists that he did not steal the egg. "I found it in a field," he exclaims. "A likely tale!" sneers the great bird. "Show us which field you mean." They obviously do not believe him. Luckily for the little bear a crow has seen what has happened, and in a few moments the sparrows and thrushes have crowded round. "Rupert didn't steal the egg," they cry, "it was here before he came to take it away."

At length the sugar birds believe that Rupert is telling the truth. After thanking the crows for their help, Rupert starts for home. To his surprise he sees the original sugar bird sitting on a post, and looking very exhausted. "Oh dear," it groans. "I'm all in, I've flown around for days searching for thieves, and I can't go on."

RUPERT GIVES A LIFT

Says Rupert, "If the way you'll show,
I'll take you where you want to go."

About the eggs he asks in vain;
The rested bird flies off again.

Then in the distance Rupert spies,
The Brothers Fox; "Hey! Wait!" he cries,

And then, "Dear me! They've run away;
That's twice they've played that trick to-day."

"You poor thing," says Rupert kindly. "Do let me help you." "I must get home," gasps the sugar bird. "Then you must let me carry you part of the way," insists the little bear. Guided by the bird he finds himself in strange country. At length they reach some high cliffs, and the sugar bird, now refreshed, leaves his arms and soars over the top.

Rupert ponders over the mystery without making anything of it. Just as he is giving it up he spies two little figures emerging from some trees down below. With excitement he recognises the Fox brothers. Perhaps they can explain things. "Hi!" he shouts, as he runs down the hill. To his amazement, when he reaches the spot the foxes have disappeared.

RUPERT LOSES HIS WAY

Thinks Rupert, "This is country queer;
Why did that bird direct me here?"

Then looking down he gets a shock;
A tunnel leads right through the rock.

The tunnel has such narrow walls,
On hands and knees he bravely crawls,

And when he comes out in the light,
He sees a fence of monstrous height.

Failing to see anything of the foxes, Rupert determines to explore the strange wood. It is full of great boulders, and is absolutely silent and deserted. With a shock he sees that a tunnel opens right at his feet and goes sloping down into the very heart of the rock. It looks very gloomy, and for a while he hesitates. Then, screwing up his courage, he steps gingerly down into the darkness.

The tunnel is very narrow and irregular, so that Rupert has to go on his hands and knees. At length he reaches the bottom, and as he starts on the upward slope the light meets him and he emerges on the other side of the cliff barrier. Before him is a huge wooden fence, which hides all the view. "My word! There must be something important behind that for anyone to build such a strong fence."

RUPERT MEETS A SOLDIER

To find an entrance he decides,
And round the fencing boldly strides;

A chocolate soldier cries, "Beware!
All Easter eggs are in my care."

The sentry shouts, the gates fly wide,
And soldiers run from every side.

Before the sugar judge he's brought,
Who says, "So, after all, you're caught."

Rupert thinks of trying to scramble up the fence, but the barbed wire on top makes him give up that idea. Running round the supports, he soon reaches a little chocolate soldier in a sentry-box, who has been gazing at him speechlessly, but who gets his voice back. "This is the home of the sugar birds and the chocolate birds," he says. "All the Easter eggs in the world come from here. But who are you? And what are you doing here?"

When he has recovered from his surprise at seeing Rupert, the sentry gives a loud shout. Instantly the gates fly open, little chocolate soldiers and sugar soldiers come running up, and the little bear finds himself hustled in front of a sugar magistrate. One of the large sugar birds is there and eyes Rupert curiously. "So they caught you after all," he says. "I thought your story was a bit weak!"

"Of Easter eggs we've been bereft;
We think you're guilty of the theft."

Then on the way to jail the bird
That Rupert helped, cries, "What's occurred?"

They find the sugar judge again,
And Rupert's honesty explain.

Then says the judge, "The tunnel show;
A soldier true with you shall go."

Rupert explains just how he got there, but the magistrate isn't satisfied. "There has been a serious theft of eggs," he says sternly, "and you're the only person we've caught so far. You will be locked up until we can find if you're speaking the truth." Suddenly there is a flutter of wings. "Why, it is Rupert!" cries a voice: "what are they doing to you?"

"This will never do," says the sugar bird. At a word from him the little soldiers march Rupert back to the sugar magistrate and the bird confirms the truth of everything that Rupert had said. "In that case," says the magistrate, "there is nothing to do but to let you go; but I do wish you would show us how you got here. We must have that tunnel blocked up." Rupert agrees.

He shows the tunnel, black as coal;
"Don't think," he says, "it's just a hole,"

"But won't you let me stay with you?
I'd like to help you find a clue."

"Well," says the soldier, "come with me;
First see our specially guarded tree.

"And now this ladder climb," he cries;
"Up there you'll get a big surprise."

Rupert points out the entrance to the tunnel. "Good gracious," says the soldier, "can one get through there?" Rupert prepares to leave for home. Then an idea strikes him and he turns suddenly. "It seems silly," he says, "to go back with the mystery still unsolved. Won't you let me stay and help you?" "Why, that's topping of you," says the chocolate soldier as he shakes his hand warmly.

"If you're going to help us you had better learn something about what goes on here," says the chocolate soldier, as he hurries Rupert through the main building. At the back a great tree comes into view. The soldier, however, finds a secret path through the spikes and hoists a ladder against the trunk. "Up you go, Rupert," he says; "there's a surprise waiting for you up there."

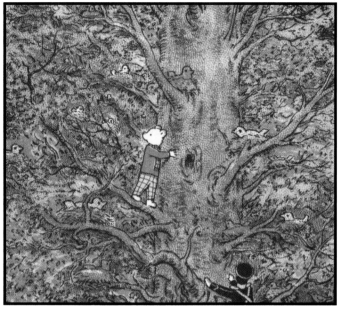

The tree is simply crammed with nests;
A sugar bird in each one rests.

A tree for chocolate birds is near,
For Easter eggs are all laid here.

"Well," says the bird upon the ground,
"Have you an explanation found?"

They haven't yet, and so explore
The sentry-guarded, locked-up store.

Half-way up the tree Rupert pauses and looks around in astonishment. The great tree is crammed with nests, and on each nest sits a sugar bird. "You see," says the little soldier, "this is where all the sugar Easter eggs come from." In the distance is another huge tree. "That," says the little man, "is where the chocolate birds live. All the chocolate eggs in the world come from there."

Descending the tree Rupert finds a gloomy-looking sugar bird waiting for him. "Well," says the bird, "I suppose the little bear hasn't found any clue?" "Not yet," says Rupert cheerfully. "I want to see where the eggs were stolen from." So the chocolate soldier takes him to the great store-rooms. "There," he says, "all the eggs are kept behind those strong doors until they're wanted for Easter."

RUPERT GETS AN IDEA

The finest eggs from every nest
Are padlocked in an iron chest.

The soldier says: "A shocking theft!"
And Rupert: "Let's spread out what's left."

Inside the chest they find a hole;
Says Rupert, "Look, through there they stole."

So off they run the fence to inspect;
That's where they'll find the great defect.

"This chest," says the soldier, "has the very finest eggs. Nobody seems to have been here—the padlocks haven't been disturbed, and yet when the chest was inspected last week half the eggs had gone!" "My word!" says Rupert, "that really is a mystery." He sits down thoroughly puzzled. Suddenly he jumps up. "I've got an idea," he cries, "let's take out all the eggs that are left."

When most of the eggs are out, Rupert points in excitement. "Just as I thought," he shouts, "the lid wasn't opened, so the eggs must have gone through the bottom—look, there's the hole that the thieves must have made!" "Why," gasps the chocolate soldier, "to do that they must have found a hole in the barricade just behind this great chest." Now they are hot on the trail and the pair run out again.

RUPERT SOLVES THE PUZZLE

Cries Rupert, "See! the fault is here."
And thinks "The Foxes have been queer."

Back through the tunnelled rock he crawls;
"Hallo!" the bird he rescued calls.

They tell their story to a crow,
Who says, "I'll show you where to go."

Inside a hut the Foxes groan;
"We ate the eggs, we're ill," they moan.

At length Rupert stops. "There you are," he cries. "That board has rotted away. The thieves must have wriggled through there and right into the back of that chest." While the chocolate soldier dashes back to spread the news, Rupert runs into the tunnel through which he had come. His thoughts fly back to the queer behaviour of the two foxes. "They must be the culprits," he mutters.

As Rupert hurries away from the tunnel he meets an old crow. He explains his haste, and the crow immediately makes him turn aside and leads him to another part of the wood where a round hut is hidden away. "The foxes have been using that hut for days," he says. Sure enough, Rupert finds what he had expected. Two sacks of lovely eggs are there and on the floor sits Freddy and Ferdy Fox.

"We've saved two sackfuls," Rupert cries;
The sugar bird for helpers flies.

Then for the Foxes Rupert begs,
"Don't punish them, they're sick of eggs."

The Foxes see the birds take wing,
Then gradually to their rescuer cling.

And Rupert's sent, on Easter Day,
The finest egg the birds could lay.

When the sugar bird sees Rupert dragging out the sacks of precious eggs it flies swiftly away, returning in a few minutes with the powerful sugar birds. "So," cries the biggest bird, "you have found the thieves. We will carry them to the sugar magistrate for punishment." "Oh, no! Please leave them alone," pleads Rupert, "they've already suffered enough and are feeling so ill. Won't you let them go?"

The sugar birds are surprised at Rupert's request, but since he has solved the mystery they agree to let the foxes go. "Oh, Rupert," says Ferdy, "what idiots we have been. But for you we might be having a dreadful time now." On Easter Day a large parcel arrives for Rupert, and in it he finds the finest sugar egg he has ever seen—a present from the sugar birds as reward for solving their mystery.

RUPERT®
and the
May Queen

RUPERT PLANS TO ATTEND THE FAIR

"Oh look at that!" cries Rupert Bear.
"Tomorrow is the Springtime Fair!"

But Gaffer Jarge wears a great frown,
There are no blossoms in the town.

Then back at home, it's time to bake
The May Fair blossom honey cake.

"Oh dear," says Mrs Bear, "I fear
We haven't any honey here."

One spring morning, Rupert and Mr Bear are out for a walk. "I say!" Rupert exclaims, as they pass a colourful poster. "Tomorrow is the Nutwood Springtime Fair!" "So it is," Mr Bear replies. Just then, their old friend Gaffer Jarge comes around the corner. Rupert waves and asks, "Are you excited about the fair?" But Gaffer Jarge frowns. "Haven't you heard?" he grumbles. "There are no spring blossoms in Nutwood. We have nothing to decorate with." Rupert and his Daddy have to get home, but they promise Gaffer Jarge that they will look for spring blossoms later that day. When they arrive back at their house, Rupert tells his Mummy about the Spring Fair. "I'd better bake a May Day cake then," she smiles, pulling out her cookbook. Rupert helps his mummy mix the ingredients, and he is feeling very cheerful until he hears Mrs Bear sigh. "Oh dear," she says, "we're all out of blossom honey."

RUPERT SEARCHES FOR BLOSSOMS

Perhaps if Rupert looks around,
The springtime blossoms can be found.

"I'll search outside," says Rupert Bear,
"For decorations for the Fair."

A passing bee is most upset,
He hasn't found the blossoms yet.

At Nutwood Common, Rupert sees
His chums out playing by the trees.

"No spring blossoms and no blossom honey? How odd!" Rupert says. He is starting to worry, but Mrs Bear says, "Never mind, Rupert. It's a beautiful day. Why don't you go and play outside?" Rupert remembers his promise to Gaffer Jarge, and thinks he'll look for spring blossoms on Nutwood Common. Mrs Bear gives him a basket to put flowers in, and Rupert sets off down the path. "I wonder if any of my chums are out this afternoon," he thinks. Suddenly, a bee whizzes past Rupert's face. "Hi there," says Rupert. "You must know where I can find some spring blossoms!" "I'm afraid not," the bee buzzes sadly. "I haven't seen any blossoms today, and I'm rather worried. We can't make honey without the nectar from blossoms, you know." Rupert wishes her luck, and continues on his way. Soon he reaches Nutwood Common, where his chums Bill Badger and Podgy Pig are enjoying the springtime weather.

RUPERT FINDS HIS CHUMS

"Oh, will you help?" he says to Bill.
His chum replies, "Of course I will."

But Podgy can't make up his mind,
And thinks he'd rather stay behind.

The pair split up to look around,
Then Rupert hears a whistling sound.

An Imp of Spring appeals to him,
"We need your help, for things are grim."

Rupert tells his pals about the shortage of spring blossoms. "Gaffer Jarge is quite upset. I wish I could help!" Then Bill has an idea. "If there are no spring blossoms this year, let's find other flowers for the May parade." "Yes, I think Gaffer Jarge would like that!" Rupert cheers. But Podgy isn't convinced. "I'd rather just sit here," he says. As Rupert and Bill head across the Common, Rupert calls back, "Well, if you change your mind . . ."

Rupert and Bill split up to cover more ground. Rupert is just bending down to pick a handful of cowslip when he hears a whistle. "What was that?" Rupert wonders. He looks around but there is nobody in sight. "Perhaps I imagined it," Rupert thinks, but then he hears a small voice call, "Look up!" Rupert peers into the branches of a nearby tree, and to his surprise, he sees an Imp of Spring. "We need your help," the Imp says. "Please come with me!"

RUPERT VISITS AN IMP

"Whatever can the trouble be?"
Asks Rupert, crawling in their tree.

"Our poor May Queen is most unwell.
She's sick in bed," the Imps do tell.

An Imp reveals their cache of seeds,
To brew the cure the May Queen needs.

Then Rupert sees they've also got
Some blossom honey in a pot.

The Imp of Spring climbs down the tree, and Rupert sees that another Imp has arrived. "This way," the second Imp says, and he points to the hollow in the tree that leads to their underground home. Rupert squeezes through the opening and climbs down the stairs. "You've heard, then, that there are no spring blossoms this year?" the Imp says miserably. "It's because our poor May Queen is ill. Without her, there will be no spring blossoms!"

The Imp explains, "Our Queen needs a special brew made from the root of a peony flower, which grows here. But she lives too far away for us to travel. Can you take it there for us?" Rupert agrees to help. As the Imps gather their ingredients, Rupert spies a familiar-looking jar. "I say, is that blossom honey?" he asks. "Oh yes, we store that down here," an Imp replies. Rupert thinks of his mother's May Day cake and asks if he can have a pot.

RUPERT TAKES THE QUEEN'S MEDICINE

"Oh, may I take one from the shelf?"
The Imps replies, "Please help yourself."

The brew will help the Queen, and then,
She'll make the blossoms grow again.

"Please take this tonic right away,
And find the Queen without delay."

So Rupert sets off on his way,
To find the poorly Queen of May.

The Imp is happy to share. "You are helping us, and we wish to help you in return!" he says gratefully. Rupert is pleased—now his Mummy will be able to make her cake! "Once the May Queen is cured and the spring blossoms come back, the bees can start making blossom honey again," the Imp says, mixing the ingredients together rapidly. "Don't forget to add a pinch of honeysuckle nectar and three spring raindrops," another Imp instructs.

The brew has turned a pretty pearly colour, and the Imp gives it one final stir. He pours it into a small vase and explains that the May Queen's nurse will need to mix it with hot water. Rupert promises to pass the instructions along. He climbs back up the stairs and crawls out of the tree. "I hope Bill hasn't worried about where I've gone," Rupert mutters. "I see your friend just over there," the Imp says, pointing. Rupert trots off towards Bill.

RUPERT AND BILL SET OFF

"Do wait up, Bill!" calls Rupert Bear.
"I have a jolly tale to share!"

He tells his chum, and Bill is keen,
To take the tonic to the Queen.

A raven flutters out to say,
"I'll lead you there—I know the way."

And with the raven as their guide,
They reach a stream that's deep and wide.

"Bill! Bill!" Rupert calls. Bill turns around in surprise, for he hadn't noticed that his friend was missing. "You'll never believe what just happened . . ." Rupert starts, and he tells Bill about his visit with the Spring Imps. But Rupert's pal doesn't believe him. "What a tale!" Bill laughs. "You do tell the best stories!" "Look at this," Rupert replies, taking out the vase of medicine. Bill stops laughing. "It is true then!" he marvels. "I'll come along with you," Bill offers. "Which way do we go?" But Rupert frowns. "I was so busy making sure I had the medicine for the Queen, I forgot to ask for directions!" Suddenly, a raven swoops down and lands on a low branch in front of them. "I have been sent to guide you to the Queen of May," she crows. The pals have to scurry along to keep up with the raven, who keeps darting this way and that, leading them deeper into the wood.

They walk along the river moss,
And use the path of stones to cross.

A fish pops up and calls, "Take care—
The May Queen needs you, Rupert Bear!"

They must be close. Then Rupert sees,
The May Queen's home amongst the trees.

They knock and stand there, side by side,
Until the grand door opens wide.

The chums soon reach a stream lined with soft, green moss. "But I don't see a bridge," Rupert muses. The raven overhears, and points her wing at a row of stones. "Yes, that's it!" Bill laughs, "the stepping-stones make the perfect bridge!" Rupert is very careful as he hops across the stones, holding the basket tightly. They reach the other side, and a fish pops his head above the water, calling, "Hurry, Rupert! The May Queen needs you!"

Rupert is relieved to see the May Queen's home come into sight. It's a beautiful palace with tall towers and arched windows. It's truly fit for the Queen of May! Rupert is feeling rather nervous as they approach the door. He and Bill stand side by side, and Rupert reaches out to knock on the big door. At first, nothing happens. "Do you think they've heard us?" Bill whispers. "I'll try again," Rupert says bravely, and this time he knocks harder.

RUPERT DELIVERS THE MEDICINE

"I'm glad you're here!" exclaims the nurse.
"Do come inside—she's getting worse."

They see the Queen asleep in bed
With flowers laced around her head.

"This tonic—from the Imps of Spring,"
The nurse cheers, "will cure anything."

The May Queen sips her drink and beams.
She's swiftly getting well, it seems.

It is the May Queen's Nurse who opens the door. Rupert hastily explains that they've been sent by the Imps of Spring to deliver medicine for the Queen. "Do come in!" the nurse smiles. "Our poor Queen has been getting worse all week. My name is Nurse Poppy." Rupert and Bill follow Nurse Poppy down the hall to a room where the May Queen is lying in bed. "Please, your highness," Rupert begins, "we've brought something for you from the Spring Imps."

Nurse Poppy takes the brew from Rupert. "This is just what we need! Now, tell me precisely how to serve the tonic." Rupert is very glad that he can recall what the Spring Imp said: "Add hot water to it." The Nurse prepares the brew in a large bowl, and soon it's ready for the Queen. As she sips the warm drink, colour starts to return to her face, and soon she is chatting animatedly with her Nurse. "The Spring Imps were spot on," Rupert thinks.

It's time to leave. For what they've done,
They've earned a bag of cakes and buns.

"I say!" cries Rupert to his chum.
"There's Podgy, looking rather glum!"

"I'm wet," he moans, "from falling in.
I will not cross those stones again."

Says Rupert Bear, "Look up ahead.
We'll take this stone bridge home instead."

Nurse Poppy thanks Rupert and Bill, and promises that she'll let them know how the Queen of May is faring. "And here is a little something for your journey home," she smiles, handing Rupert a thick bag filled with cakes, iced buns and jam tarts. The chums begin their walk home along the path. Suddenly, Bill exclaims, "Look! It's Podgy!" And there is poor Podgy, standing on the path, dripping with water and looking quite cold and miserable.

"I followed your path, only I slipped and fell in the stream," Podgy whimpers. "You'll soon dry off," Bill says, but Podgy is still upset. "The stones are slippery, and I won't cross them again!" Rupert looks around, and spies an old, wooden sign. "The letters are a bit faded, but I can read the word 'BRIDGE'. Let's go this way." Just then, their friend the raven flies down. "Be careful if you cross," she warns. "The bridge is a troll bridge."

The raven murmurs, "Have a care."
For it's a Troll Bridge! Do they dare?

A troll looms out! They hear him say,
"You shall not cross, unless you pay!"

"We have no coins for you to take,"
Says Rupert, "Only buns and cake."

The troll's delighted. "Are you sure?
No one has brought me cake before!"

Rupert and Bill aren't sure, but Podgy refuses to go back any other way. "It's such an old sign," Bill says hopefully, "perhaps there isn't a troll anymore." The chums approach the bridge cautiously, but no one is in sight. Suddenly, Rupert hears heavy footsteps. "Quick, let's turn back!" he calls, but it's too late! A giant troll looms out. "Do you dare to disturb me and my bridge?" he bellows. "None shall cross unless they have paid the fee!"

"Please, we haven't any money," Rupert tells the troll. "We didn't mean to disturb you. We were calling upon the Queen of May, only our friend slipped and fell into the river. He's cold and wet and we must get him home quickly." Then Rupert has an idea. "Why don't you take these lovely cakes instead?" The troll's scowl vanishes, and he doesn't look so fearsome anymore! "C-c-cakes? For m-m-me? Nobody has ever brought me c-c-cakes before!"

RUPERT MAKES A FRIEND

The troll is kind, though awfully shy,
And takes them to his home to dry.

The troll brings out a cup of tea,
Which Podgy sips quite happily.

"I'm sorry that I was so rude,"
The troll says, as they share their food.

And soon the healthy May Queen comes,
To take home Rupert and his chums.

The troll apologises for being rude, and explains that he lives all alone in the woods and isn't used to having visitors. "My house is just over there. You could come and dry off." Rupert and his chums realise that the troll isn't cruel at all, only a bit lonely. So they follow him up the path to a large, brick house. Inside, there is a roaring fire and big, plush chairs. Podgy is already feeling much happier, and the troll brings large mugs of tea.

Rupert shares the cakes and tells the troll about their visit with the May Queen. The troll knows the Queen and is glad to hear that she is getting better. Just then, there is a knock on the door. It's the May Queen herself! "How are you, Your Highness?" Rupert asks. And the May Queen replies, "Much better indeed!" Then she smiles at the troll and says, "Hello, my old friend. I think it's time that I take these three adventurers back to Nutwood!"

RUPERT FLIES HOME

The May Queen's giant hare can fly,
And pulls her carriage through the sky.

They soar along and as they go,
The blossoms flourish down below.

A Spring Imp waves and starts to cheer,
He's thrilled the blooms are finally here.

They land by Rupert's family,
Who greet their son quite happily.

The May Queen promises to visit the troll again soon, so he won't be so lonely. Then she takes the chums outside. There, out in front, is her carriage . . . and in the harness is a giant hare! "Back to Nutwood!" the May Queen calls with a twinkle in her eye, and the giant hare leaps up into the sky. "We're flying!" Rupert gasps, peering over the edge. Below, he sees wild flowers blooming to life. "They must be spring blossoms," Rupert thinks.

"Look!" Rupert says excitedly. "It's an Imp of Spring!" He calls down, and the Spring Imp waves back. "We knew you could do it!" the Imp cheers. "We knew you'd save our Queen of May!" The carriage flies on, and in no time at all, they arrive at Rupert's house. As they land, Mr and Mrs Bear come out. "Oh, there you are, Rupert. We wondered what you'd been up to," says Mr Bear. "You do get up to the most astonishing things," Mrs Bear adds.

RUPERT SAYS GOODBYE

The Queen of May tells Rupert Bear,
"Now here's a gift for you to share."

She bids her new-found friends goodbye,
As they take off into the sky.

When Rupert Bear unwraps his box,
He sees the little wooden stalks.

The sticks make music when they're played.
They're perfect for the May parade!

Rupert invites his new friends to stay, but the May Queen says that she must continue flying around Nutwood, restoring the spring blossoms. "I have a gift for you and your friends, Rupert Bear," she smiles, and hands him a small parcel. Rupert watches her leave, and spots Gaffer Jarge off in the distance. Their old friend is cheering too. "I'm so pleased that Gaffer Jarge will have his spring blossoms in time for the Springtime Fair!" he says.

Podgy has to go home, and Rupert says that he'll see him tomorrow. Then he and Bill look at the parcel. "Let's open it!" Bill says. So Rupert slowly unwraps the box. Inside are a set of saplings carved into little whistles that can play music. "What a jolly thing!" Rupert marvels. He and Bill each take a whistle and practise playing. "I should be off too," Bill says finally. "But it's been quite a day, hasn't it? First you saw the Spring Imps . . ."

RUPERT BRINGS BACK HONEY

Then Rupert says, *"Look what I've brought!"*
And gives his Mum the honey pot.

"It's blossom honey for my cake,"
Cheers Mrs Bear. "Now I can bake!"

The May Fair is delightful fun,
With cake and dance for everyone!

"Oh what a jolly Springtime Fair
In Nutwood," whistles Rupert Bear.

"The Imps of Spring . . . I'd almost forgotten!" Rupert says to his Mummy. "I know why we were out of blossom honey—the May Queen was too ill to make blossoms, so the bees couldn't make any more honey. But the Imps of Spring keep a supply of blossom honey." He gives the pot to Mrs Bear, who is delighted. It's getting late, but there's just enough time to bake a cake. "There!" Mrs Bear cheers. "Now we'll have a May Day honey blossom cake to share!"

The next morning, the Bears head over to the Springtime Fair. The parade has already begun, and Rupert waves to all his chums. Mrs Bear puts her honey blossom cake out on the table, and in no time at all, everyone gathers round to try a slice. "Who'd have thought that I nearly couldn't make this!" she laughs. "Thank you, Rupert, and thanks to the Spring Imps for the honey!" Rupert grins. "I think this is the best Springtime Fair we've ever had!"

Spot the Difference

Rupert and his chums are having a wonderful time at the Springtime Fair.
There are 7 differences between the two pictures. Can you spot them all?

Answers: The troll has disappeared, the raven has turned into a Sugar Bird, the church has disappeared, Ferdy's jacket has turned from red to green, Willie Mouse has swapped places with Rupert, a hedgehog has appeared, a bee has appeared.

Your Own Rupert Story

Why not try colouring the pictures below and writing a story to fit them? Write your story in four parts, one for each picture, saying what it shows. Then, faintly in pencil, print each part neatly on the lines under its picture. When they fit, go over the printing with a pen. There is space at the top of the page for a title.

RUPERT

and the

CORAL ISLAND

Silverstrand is a lovely spot for a holiday, as Rupert soon discovers. But the little bear hardly has time to settle down before he is taken on a surprise trip far across the ocean. It leads to some strange adventures in a very secret place, and Rupert is able to prove the old Bosun's yarns are not fairy tales.

"I think," says Mr Bear one day,
"You both deserve a holiday."

Sighs Rupert, pacing to and fro,
"I really don't know where to go."

Then Rupert hears the sailor shout,
"What are you worrying about?"

The Bosun smiles, "Just take my tip,
I know the best place for your trip."

"Look, Rupert," says Mr Bear one day. "I should like you and your Mummy to have a week's holiday, so I've brought a lot of papers about seaside places. Let's see which is the nicest." "These pictures all make them look lovely," murmurs Mrs Bear, "but I don't think any of them can be nicer than our old favourites, Sandy Bay and Rocky Bay. I'll leave it to Rupert and we'll go wherever he chooses." So, feeling very important, the little bear walks slowly around, trying to decide which place his Mummy would enjoy the most. All at once Rupert is startled by a cheerful shout. "Hi, little bear, why so thoughtful? Come and meet my old shipmate, the Bosun." "It's Sailor Sam!" cries Rupert, running over the grass. "I was thoughtful because my Mummy's going to take me to the sea and I can't decide whether to go to Rocky Bay or Sandy Bay." "Those are good places," declares the Bosun. "But take my advice and go to neither of them!"

RUPERT STAYS TO LISTEN

The old man adds, "Try Silverstrand,
If you like rocks and lots of sand."

"What thrilling stories he must tell!
I'd like to hear his tales as well."

Then Rupert listens eagerly
Until it's almost time for tea.

Shouts Rupert, running down the track,
"Hooray! I just can't wait to pack!"

Seeing Rupert's surprise the old Bosun explains his meaning. "Sandy Bay has lovely sands and Rocky Bay has lovely rocks," he says, "But I live between them at Silverstrand which has plenty of both and is the best seaside place I know, although I have been all round the world!" "All round the world?" Rupert is thrilled. "What stories you must tell!" "Yes," laughs Sailor Sam. "You must ask him for his tales of the Coral Islands. You've never heard any like them." "Oo, yes please!" cries the little bear. The old Bosun's stories are so enthralling that Rupert wants him to go on and on, but Sailor Sam declares that it is time for tea. "Dear, dear, so it is," says the old man. "We must stop. But I've taken a fancy to you, little bear, so if you'll come and see me on your holiday I'll tell you more about the Coral Islands. I live in a shack on the cliffs." Rupert is delighted and scampers home to tell his Mummy that he has decided on Silverstrand.

Laughs Daddy, "That's a good idea!
Look, this is Silverstrand, just here."

So they decide to go by rail,
And Rupert takes his spade and pail.

Guide Pauline finds them on the train,
And says, "It's nice to meet again!"

"I'm off to camp," explains the Guide,
And settles down by Rupert's side.

When he hears that Rupert has made up his mind Mr Bear gets out a map and finds the chosen place. "None of us has ever been to Silverstrand," he says. "It is a very good idea. I only wish I could come with you." The preparations for the holiday and the packing cause some bustle and excitement, but after a day or two it is done and then Mr Bear takes Rupert and his Mummy to Nutwood station. At the town of Nutchester Rupert and his mother have changed from their slow train into one with a corridor and now they are speeding towards the sea. All at once the little bear sees someone walking past his window. "Why, surely that's Pauline, one of our village Girl Guides!" he cries. "Hi, Pauline, come and talk to us. Where are you going?" "I'm going to my pals," says Pauline as she joins them. "They're camping at Silverstrand." "How topping!" exclaims Rupert. "That's the very place we're heading for. We'll be there together! It will be such fun!"

RUPERT LIKES THE BEACH

They leave their luggage to the man,
Though Rupert carries what he can.

Cries Rupert, "What a lovely view!
I do like Silverstrand, don't you?"

"Now here's some rock, don't eat it all,"
Says Mummy, as they leave the stall.

So Rupert runs across the shore,
To see his sailor friend once more.

When the train arrives at Silverstrand everybody gets busy. Mrs Bear arranges for the luggage to be taken to the boarding house, Pauline collects her things and says goodbye as she starts for camp, while Rupert carries what he can. After they have settled in and have had their tea Mrs Bear takes Rupert to a cliff-top to see the view. "I say, what a wonderful place!" cries the little bear. "Look at those stretches of hard, flat sand with lovely broken strips of rock between them. No wonder the old Bosun is so fond of it!" Next day Rupert asks permission to call on the old Bosun. "He's promised to tell me more stories of his adventures on the Coral Islands," he says. "I should like to take him a present. D'you think he would enjoy a stick of Silverstrand rock?" Mrs Bear is not quite sure, but she buys him a piece of rock from a tiny shop below the promenade and sends him off. "I hope I can remember the old man's directions," he murmurs as he trots along the sands.

RUPERT CALLS ON THE BOSUN

Between the cliffs a path is cut,
It leads towards the Bosun's hut.

"I've got a sail to mend, you see,"
The Bosun says, "so sit by me."

"Hullo," smiles Rupert, "look who's come!
It's Beryl—she is Pauline's chum."

A thrilling yarn the old man spins,
"'Twas in the South Seas . . ." he begins.

Rupert finds his friends. "Hello, here I am!" he calls cheerily. "May I join you? What a topping shack you have here." "Why, Rupert!" cries the Bosun heartily. "Come along and sit by me. I'm just repairing a sail for the Girl Guides from your village. When that's done you shall hear more of my tales of the Coral Isles. I'm sure that's what you've come for." So Rupert perches himself happily beside him and waits. When the sail is finished Rupert offers his piece of Silverstrand rock, but the old Bosun smiles and refuses it. "No thank'ee. That sweet stuff is no good to old men," he says. "Now if that had been real South Sea rock from my Coral Islands . . ." At that moment a new figure appears. It is Beryl, another Guide. "Oh, are you spinning yarns again?" she cries. "Do let me listen, too." So for the next hour the Bosun tells his young friends many tales of wonder, of sparkling seas, of mermaids, and flying fishes, and of faraway magic lands bathed in sunlight.

RUPERT ENJOYS THE TALE

Smiles Beryl, "I enjoyed that tale,
Well, now I'll carry back the sail."

"Your coral islands sound such fun
That I should like to visit one."

As Rupert starts to scramble down,
A Guide is coming back from town.

"But," Janet smiles, "those yarns aren't real!
They're simply fairy tales, I feel."

At length Beryl pulls herself together. "I must get back to the others or they'll think I'm lost," she declares. But Rupert stays behind and looks wistfully at his old friend. "Oo, how I wish I could see a coral island!" he says. "D'you think I'll ever be clever enough to find one?" The old man smiles at him. "My sort of coral island can't be found by being clever," he murmurs. "Nor even by being a good sailor, but only by being born under a lucky star!" Rupert is strangely excited by the Bosun's stories, and as he goes home he ponders on what he has heard, though there is much he cannot understand. On reaching the sand he meets a small figure carrying supplies from the town. It is Janet, yet another of the Girl Guides, and, offering her a piece of his sweet, he tells her of the old man's coral islands and the real South Sea rock on them. But she only seems amused. "The Bosun's tales are lovely," she smiles. "They must be only fairy tales!"

RUPERT CARRIES SOME SHOPPING

"Perhaps," says Rupert, "but I find
Those stories still stay in my mind."

"Look," Rupert cries, "there is a boat!
But surely it can't be afloat!"

Gasps Rupert, "Where's the boat we've seen?
And what do these strange furrows mean?"

"We made the boat with odds and ends,"
Says Janet as they watch the friends.

Although Janet has laughed at them, Rupert cannot get the old man's stories out of his mind as he offers to help her carry her shopping over the ridge of rock. Beyond it is a stretch of sand and then another ridge over which he spies a sail. "Hello, there's a boat," he calls. "That must be Beryl's sail on it. How near it looks. What is it sailing on? I didn't know the sea was just the other side of those rocks." "Neither did I," chuckles Janet mysteriously, "because it isn't!" Feeling baffled by what Janet has said Rupert climbs over the second ridge of rock. "You're quite right," he says. "There is no sea here, only hard sand with marks on it. What can it mean?" In another moment the puzzle is solved. Three more Guides come into sight pulling a strange object along, some long light planks, a mast and a sail, all mounted on two pairs of wheels. "There, now you see our secret," Janet smiles. "It's a sandboat. We've made it ourselves. Don't you think it's grand?"

RUPERT STEERS THE SANDBOAT

"Oo! May I try your sandboat, please?"
Begs Rupert. "There's a lovely breeze!"

While Rupert steers, away they skim.
"Well done!" the girls call after him.

But when the sandboat hits a rock
Pauline is flung off by the shock.

The sandboat swerves as if to crash,
Then hits the water with a splash.

Rupert is thrilled by the sandboat. "I say, you are clever!" he exclaims. "Did you really make it yourselves? D'you think I might have a ride on it?" "We're not really very clever," Beryl smiles. "At present it only goes with the wind right behind it. That's why you saw us pulling back by hand. But you shall have a ride if you like. You can steer and Pauline shall control the sail." They turn the sandboat and, with Rupert aboard, start it on its way. Rupert has difficulty in guiding the sandboat clear of obstacles, so Pauline makes fast the sail cords in order to leave her hands free to help him steer. As she does so the little craft hits a boulder with a violent bump and before she can save herself the Guide is jolted right off. Rupert manages to stay on board, but next moment the freshening breeze has driven the sandboat into the sea and as it meets the water he is pitched forward near to the mast. "Oo! It was my fault for not steering properly!" he gasps in dismay.

RUPERT DRIFTS OUT TO SEA

"You'll soon drift back," the Girl Guides shout,
"Because the tide's not going out."

Then Rupert says, "It's deep, I think,
I hope the boat's not going to sink."

Cries Rupert, "Come and rescue me
Before I drift right out to sea!"

But help is close at hand instead,
For soon he sees the Merboy's head.

The Girl Guides are startled to see what has happened. Running to Pauline they make sure that she is not hurt and then they shout to Rupert, "Lower the sail, lower the sail! The tide will bring you in again!" Feeling very dazed, the little bear stumbles forward, but by the time he has discovered what to do he is on the wrong side of the mast and the sail comes down on top of him. "This is dreadful!" he gasps. "We must be in deep water. I do hope we're not going to sink!"

To keep the sail out of the water Rupert fixes it slightly up. The result is that the wind still catches it and drifts him further from the shore. Desperately he shouts, hoping the Guides will try to get a boat to rescue him. All at once a voice quite near at hand makes him hurry to the other side of the sandboat. A cheery little face has appeared from the waves. "Why, you're a Merboy, aren't you?" cries Rupert. "I am glad to see you! Can you help me out of this fix and get me ashore?"

RUPERT WAITS FOR THE MERBOY

Says Rupert, standing near the mast,
"We tried to sail the boat too fast."

The Merboy smiles, "I'll find a fish
Who'll take you anywhere you wish."

Thinks Rupert, "This will hold, I hope."
And makes a big loop in the rope.

The Merboy swims below to ask
A fish to do a special task.

The Merboy flips himself on board the sandboat. "Now then, what's up?" he demands. "I've never seen a craft like this. And what was all that shouting about?" Rupert rapidly explains how he has come to be on the sea and how the Guides made the strange boat. The Merboy grins happily. "Well, don't worry," he says. "I'll get a fish to pull you home. No trouble at all." He tells Rupert just how to prepare for the arrival of the fish, then he dives gracefully into the waves. Rupert tries to remember just what the Merboy told him to do. Putting his hand into the water he manages to untie the steering rope. Then he makes a loop in one end and fixes the other firmly to the forestay. "Well, there's one good thing," he murmurs, "We don't look like sinking. I suppose there must be lots of air in those tyres to make the sandboat float so high." Meanwhile, unknown to him, the Merboy is swimming below the waves. He searches about until he finds a messenger fish.

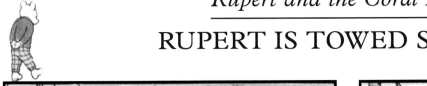

"If what the Merboy says is true,
The fish should know just what to do."

"Why did the fish dash off like that?"
Gasps Rupert, as he tumbles flat.

"Come back! Come back!" the Guides exclaim,
But Rupert streaks out just the same.

The boat goes racing on at speed,
And Rupert's very scared indeed.

Rupert has barely finished his preparations when the surface of the sea is broken and the head of a huge fish appears and stares silently. "Oh dear, he looks awfully fierce and not very brainy," thinks the little bear. "I hope he knows what to do." The Merboy shows no signs of returning, so he throws the rope. Catching the loop, the fish turns in a flash, and dashes away with the sandboat so violently that Rupert is again toppled over and covered with salt spray. Two of the Guides have run to find a boat to rescue Rupert, while the others wait hoping he will drift in. Suddenly Janet gives a shout. "Look, he's not coming in! He's going further out, and he's going faster! What on earth can be happening?" Although the Guides cannot see the fish, it is now going so fast that the front of the sandboat is lifted above the water. On goes the little craft, past the great Gull Rock, away from the shore and out towards the wide ocean until Silverstrand has faded from sight.

He's all alone and far from land,
And longs to be at Silverstrand.

Says Rupert, "Here's a calmer spot
It's night-time, yet it's very hot."

At dawn he rouses from his sleep,
And sees the rocks so sharp and steep.

Says Rupert, "It is very queer
To find the rocks so spiky here."

The great fish swims so powerfully, sometimes on the surface and sometimes under water, that all land is soon out of sight. Poor Rupert can do nothing about it but cling to the mast as screaming gulls wheel around him inquisitively. "The Merboy said that the fish would pull me home," he thinks miserably. "But where am I now?" He becomes very tired, but as evening approaches the sea gets calmer and he finds himself passing more slowly between small, weird shaped islands. When at last the sandboat stops, darkness has fallen. The night has become very warm, and as Rupert can see nothing at all he lies down thankfully and sleeps. At length the dawn awakens him, and he gazes around at islands of the oddest shapes. The fish has disappeared so, pulling up the tow rope, he tosses the loop over a jagged piece of the nearest island. Soon he is clambering ashore. "Ow, what queer rock this is!" he exclaims, rubbing his knuckles. "Some of it is all spiky and sharp!"

He murmurs, "It's a lovely place.
Whichever way I turn and face."

"This really is the strangest sight,"
Cries Rupert, peering at the light.

"Perhaps some creature lives below,"
Thinks Rupert. "I would like to know."

"There's no one here except myself,
But someone's put these on the shelf."

As the light grows brighter the islands seem to become more fantastic in shape, and in the rays of the sun they glow with all the colours of the rainbow. "What a perfectly lovely place," Rupert whispers as he clambers upward over rock that is partly hard and partly soft, "and what gorgeous flowers! How do they grow here, where there is no soil?" Moving still higher he spies a deep crack leading into the depths of the island. "There's light down there!" he mutters. "How very odd!"

There seems to be nobody on the strange island. No birds are flying and there is only silence all around. "I wonder if anybody lives down there," thinks Rupert, peering into the cleft. Cautiously letting himself over the edge, he finds that there are rough steps at the sides and soon he emerges into a beautiful cave with a deep pool in the middle. As he glances about him he sees a row of shells on a shelf. "Those didn't get there by accident," he cries. "Somebody must live here!"

RUPERT CANNOT FIND HIS WAY

He tastes a nut that's greenish brown,
The bitter flavour makes him frown!

Then suddenly a fish leaps high
Above the rocky pool near by.

So lonely, Rupert sighs, "I wish
That I could see that little fish."

Dismayed, he says, "Where am I now?
I must have lost my way somehow."

Rupert sees that each of the large shells contains what seems to be some kind of food and he suddenly realises how long it is since he had anything to eat. "My, I'm hungry!" he thinks, choosing what looks like a greeny brown nut and biting it. Next instant he pulls a wry face. "Ugh, that was horrid!" he cries. "All salty and bitter." As he turns away in disappointment there is a movement in the dark pool opposite the shells, and a small fish leaps high out of the water. Giving one startled glance, the fish flops back into the water and disappears into the depths. "That's the first moving thing I've seen since I arrived," says Rupert. "I wish it would come back." But the fish does not return, so he climbs up through the cleft and out into the open air. Now a fresh problem meets him, for the island is such a mass of odd shapes that he cannot remember which way he first came. "And I can't see the boat either," he says, becoming more and more anxious.

RUPERT FEELS SO LONELY

Across the waters of the bay
The boat is drifting far away.

Wails Rupert, feeling very sad,
"There goes the only chance I had!"

But presently comes someone's shout,
"Hi, what is all this noise about?"

"This island's private, is that clear?
You have no business being here."

After scrambling over the lovely island and amongst its rocks, some very hard and sharp, Rupert rounds a corner and gives a gasp of dismay. The tide has risen, lifting the rope from where it was fixed, and the precious sandboat is drifting out into the calm, open sea. In desperation he shouts for help, but there is no reply. Again there is only silence and he begins to lose hope. Lying down he tries to think. "What ever can I do now?" he moans. "I don't even know where I am. I'm completely lost." Rupert racks his brains for some way of escape, without success. Then, to his astonishment, a voice quite near him calls out, "What's all the shouting about? Who has dared to come here?" Starting up, Rupert sees that it is his friend the Merboy, now looking not at all friendly, but frowning at him. "Oh, how glad I am to see you!" Rupert cries. "H'm, so it's you again!" says the Merboy. "A little fish told me someone was here. Go away, it's private!"

The little bear says, "Don't blame me,
Your big fish brought me here, you see!"

"That fish is stupid, though he's strong,"
The Merboy laughs, "and he was wrong!"

"I've only had a nut to chew,"
Says Rupert, "so I'll follow you."

Then Rupert thinks it is a treat
To find such lovely rock to eat.

Eagerly Rupert explains how the great fish pulled him on the sandboat and left him stranded. At first the Merboy looks puzzled, then he loses his frown and to Rupert's relief he breaks into a merry laugh. "I see it all now," he chuckles. "That fish is very strong, but he is not very clever. I told him to take you home, and instead of taking you to your home he has brought you to my home! How frightened you must have been. And jolly hungry, too!" At the Merboy's words Rupert realises that he is hungrier than ever. "I found some things in your big shells but they tasted awfully queer," he says timidly. "Ha-ha, I'll give you something better," laughs the Merboy as he leads the way to another cave. "You've noticed that there are all kinds of rock here. Some of it in there is even eatable. Try a bit." Rupert breaks off a piece nervously. "M-m-m, this is scrumptious!" he cries. "I say, can this be real South Sea rock that the Bosun spoke of in his yarns?"

RUPERT'S FRIEND COMES BACK

"It won't be difficult at all,"
The Merboy says, and blows a call.

The flying fishes hear the sound,
And quickly they come darting round.

While Rupert's at the water-side,
The boat drifts closer on the tide.

Up comes the Merboy with some weed,
Which is the very thing they need.

The Merboy tells Rupert to eat his fill of the delicious South Sea rock and to fill his pockets with it. When his hunger is satisfied the little bear says that he must recover the sandboat. "It belongs to my pals, the Guides," he says. "They will want it back." "That's easy," declares the Merboy. Picking up a shell, he blows a long weird note on it. Next moment a shoal of flying fishes are darting around. He murmurs some strange words to them, then dives into the sea and they all make off.

Rupert watches anxiously, and for a while nothing seems to happen. The Merboy is under water and the flying fishes have disappeared. Then he realises that the sandboat is drifting towards instead of away from him. When it is quite near to the island there is a sudden swell and the Merboy bobs up out of the sea. In one hand he holds many lengths of tough seaweed. "Now, little bear, jump aboard as soon as you can," he calls cheerily. "Then we shan't be long getting you home!"

RUPERT REACHES SILVERSTRAND

"Although this weed is hard to grip,
I'll tie a knot that will not slip."

Away they sail, and soon they find
The island has been left behind.

Says Janet, "Quick, just look out there!
It's our sandboat—and Rupert Bear!"

The Merboy's left his little friend
Now that the journey's at an end.

Once Rupert is back on the sandboat the Merboy heaves the seaweed on board. "Now then, untie your rope from the forestay and fix this stuff in its place," he orders. It is not easy, for the seaweed is slippery, but by gripping one end of all the strands Rupert at length makes a secure knot. Then the flying fishes return and seem to know just what to do. Each one seizes a strand and in a moment the sandboat is speeding away, leaving the many-coloured island gleaming in the sunlight behind.

Rupert's disappearance has caused great excitement at Silverstrand. All evening search parties have scoured the seas without finding him, and next morning the Guides are out again fearing that he may be wrecked on the Gull Rock. As they head homeward in the late afternoon Pauline gives a sudden shout. "Look, look, there he is! Just where we saw him yesterday!" The Merboy sees them coming and with a hasty farewell, he dives overboard and the little bear sees him no more.

Their speedboat follows back to land,
As out jumps Rupert on the sand.

"How lucky!" Rupert laughs. "Hooray!
I'm back where I was yesterday."

The fish turn quickly from the shore,
And fly away to sea once more.

Across the sand the Girl Guides come
To welcome home their little chum.

The flying fishes obey their orders and, in spite of the Merboy's sudden departure, they make straight for the land. The speedboat, with the three Guides calling excitedly, gains on Rupert rapidly but has to veer away for fear of running into the shallows. Once the wheels of the sandboat touch the sand the fishes drop their towing lines and turn back towards the open sea while Rupert leaps ashore. "How marvellous," he laughs. "This is the very spot I started from yesterday." As the speedboat swerves away from the shallows there is a squeal from Janet. The flying fishes, having finished their job, are heading out to sea again. "What can they be?" gasps Pauline. In a moment they are gone and the boat roars away to the jetty. Meanwhile, Rupert finds he can just drag the sandboat above the high-tide mark. Then he clambers over the rocks, and waves to the Guides who have landed from their speedboat and are running eagerly to meet him.

RUPERT AMAZES HIS MUMMY

*"When I've found Mummy, I won't fail
To tell you my exciting tale."*

*Smiles Beryl, "Rupert's safe and well,
But where he's been I cannot tell."*

*When Mrs Bear has had some rock,
She soon recovers from the shock.*

*"Let's tell the Bosun what I've done!"
Says Rupert, so away they run.*

The Guides are astonished to see Rupert looking none the worse for his long absence and they want to ask dozens of questions all together. Rupert tries to tell them, then he stops. "No, I must go to Mummy first," he declares. "She's sure to be worrying about me." So Beryl races away to find Mrs Bear and tell her the good news while Rupert, who cannot run so fast, follows with Pauline and Janet, and they all meet at the promenade. Mrs Bear is so relieved that she feels quite faint, so the Guides take her to a shelter while she listens to the whole strange story. Finally, Rupert asks her to try a piece of the South Sea rock he has brought so far. "My, that's delicious!" she sighs. "I feel better already. And now let's go home." But Rupert begs to be allowed to tell the old Bosun. Mrs Bear looks anxious again. "Very well, but come straight back to me," she says, at length. "Don't let that old man keep you too long, Rupert." And the little friends scamper happily away.

RUPERT PROVES THE YARNS

He climbs up to the Bosun's shack,
And calls out, "Hallo! I've come back!"

The Bosun mutters, "Aye, this stuff
Came from my islands sure enough!"

He whispers, "Then it's really true!
And now I know it, thanks to you!"

So Rupert turns to wave his hands
Then hurries home across the sands.

The old Bosun turns in surprise. "Why, young Rupert, they told me you were missing," he cries. "Where've 'ee bin?" The little bear hastens to explain everything, and he produces another piece of the strange rock. "And now, please do tell me," he pleads, "was that island I went to one of the coral islands in your story? And is this the South Sea rock that you told us about?" Rupert waits for an answer, but the old man is staring in silent amazement. "'Tis true, 'tis all true," he whispers.

At last the old Bosun finds his voice. "Little bear, you've done a great thing for me this day!" he cries. "For years my stories of coral islands have been getting stranger and stranger until I hardly knew whether to believe them myself. But now you've been there, why bless 'ee, they must all be true!" He laughs in glee, and, feeling very happy, the little friends go on their way, Rupert back to his Mummy and the Guides to see if their sand-boat still goes well after its adventure.

RUPERT
and the
TURNIPS

How a sneeze caused
the loss of a valuable
locket and the peculiar
place in which it was
found.

RUPERT RUNS AN ERRAND

"You've lost your brooch," cries Rupert Bear,
"Perhaps it's in the house somewhere."

At length the missing brooch is found,
In mother's wash-tub, safe and sound.

Says Mr Bear, "This catch won't do."
So Rupert says, "I'll go for you."

Then Mr Rabbit asks the bear
If he has any time to spare.

Rupert, tired of playing by himself, comes in and watches Mrs Bear. All at once he gives a little cry of surprise and points. "Your brooch," says Rupert. "You had it on at breakfast." "Good gracious," cries Mrs Bear, feeling at her neck, "it's dropped somewhere." Rupert looks carefully on every floor, but has no luck. "Oh, dear, I simply can't lose that brooch," she moans; "it belonged to your great-grandmother." Suddenly she snatches one hand away. "Something pricked me," she cries. Then she pulls out a sheet and there is the missing brooch.

Mrs Bear is overjoyed at finding her brooch. "It will have to be mended," says Rupert. "May I run to the jeweller's with it? Then I could see if my pal Algy could come out to play." Soon the little bear is trotting happily along the road into Nutwood. Reaching the village, Rupert takes the brooch into the jeweller's shop. "That can easily be mended," says Mr Rabbit. "Are you running any more errands for your mother?" he asks. "If not, you can do something important for me!" "Oh yes," cries Rupert, "I'd love to. Do tell me what I have to do."

RUPERT ASKS THE WAY

"This locket must not come to harm,
It's Mrs Brown's down at the farm."

Quite soon he meets his little chum,
And Algy asks, "Please may I come?"

Old Gaffer Jarge says, "Now you two;
You're trespassing. Be off with you!"

To Farmer Brown's he points the way,
But says, "They're in the fields to-day."

Mr Rabbit puts a small parcel into Rupert's hands. "That is a valuable locket that I have been repairing," he says. "It belongs to Mrs Brown, wife of Farmer Brown. I want you to take it very carefully to Mrs Brown herself." Rupert is thrilled to have such an important errand. He puts the locket safely into his pocket and starts on his way. As he crosses the first field he spies a little figure on a fence. "Why, it's Algy!" he cries. "I was going to call for you when Mr Rabbit gave me an important job." He tells his pal about the locket for Mrs Brown.

Near a gate they suddenly meet the ancient Gaffer Jarge, Farmer Wurzel's grandfather. "Now then," growls the old man, "what be you young varmints up to? Trespassing for blackberries, I'll be bound. Just you be off." Gaffer Jarge looks at Rupert and Algy carefully. "I seldom see any of you young folks when you're not up to some sort of mischief," he grunts. Leaning on a fence, the ancient man points with his stick. "It's no good going to Farmer Brown's house," he says. "He and all his people are in the fields over that hill."

RUPERT GETS A RIDE

A little farther on they spy
A cart that is with corn piled high.

"There's no one here," cries little bear;
"Let's climb on top and wait up there."

The driver comes and off they go,
But they're asleep and do not know.

And when at last the cart does stop
The driver finds the chums on top.

The two friends set off in the direction indicated by Gaffer Jarge. Over the hill they go and through meadows until Rupert suddenly stops. "Look, there's a harvest cart pointing the other way," says Rupert. "It must be Farmer Brown's." Feeling that their journey is nearly over they trot towards it. Rupert and Algy reach the farm cart laden with corn, but to their surprise there is still nobody in sight. "Let's get on top of the load," suggests Algy. "It should be cosy up there." It is not too easy, but they both manage it without hurting themselves.

The day is warm, and their new bed is so comfortable that they both doze off. Sam, the farmhand, comes back, perches on the cart, and drives away; but Rupert and Algy know nothing about it. At length Rupert stirs and blinks his eyes. Then he remembers and nudges Algy, who sits up suddenly. "Where are we?" he asks. "How long have we been asleep?" "Who's that talking?" asks a voice from below. The cart stops, and the astonished face of Sam appears. "Good morning," says Rupert cheerfully. "We've come to pay a call on Mrs Brown."

RUPERT HELPS TO HARVEST

He crossly tells them to get down,
Then takes them off to Farmer Brown.

The farmer says his wife is out,
So they decide to wait about.

Then Rupert says, "What can we do?
For while we wait we can help you."

So armed with sickles off they go,
And round the oats a path they mow.

Rupert and Algy burst out laughing at the surprise on Sam's face. He leads the two little pals through a field of turnips to where Farmer Brown is standing and explains where he found them. Rupert's story is soon told. Farmer Brown smiles broadly. "My wife has gone to the village, and won't be back for an hour or so," he says. "You can give me the locket." But Rupert puts his hand into his pocket. "No," he says. "Mr Rabbit said that I was to give it to Mrs Brown and to nobody else." "You're a very trustworthy person, so I won't argue," says the farmer.

Seeing that they have some time to wait for the return of Mrs Brown the farmer suggests that the two friends do some of the farm work, and gets them a couple of sickles. "I have a field of oats," he says, "and I want the edge of it cut so as to leave room for the machine to get in and finish the job." "My, aren't they sharp?" says Rupert, as he feels the edges of the sickles. "Well, mind you don't swing round too fast and cut off your own feet!" smiles the farmer. "I'm going to start with the scythe now. You can go round the field in the opposite direction."

It's very hot and such hard work,
But they're determined not to shirk.

The Farmer's pleased they did not slack,
And says, "Wait here till I get back."

Then while they wait the little bear
Unwraps the locket with great care.

Cries Algy, "Let me hold it, please."
Then drops it when he gives a sneeze!

Cutting the oats proves such hot work that it is not long before the two friends are out of breath. They keep on steadily, although they get more out of breath, but before they have cut forty yards the farmer appears after cutting all the rest of the edge. They sit down wondering what he will say. To the surprise of Rupert and Algy, Farmer Brown seems quite pleased with them. "You've done very well," says the Farmer. "If Mrs Brown is home I'll ask her to bring you some lunch. Then you can give her that precious packet in your pocket."

"Now, Rupert," says Algy, "show me that locket before Mrs Brown comes." Rupert takes the small packet from his pocket and unwraps it very carefully. Algy begs to be allowed to hold the precious locket. "All right; just for a minute," says Rupert. "But we must wrap it up again before Mrs Brown Turnes." And he hands it over. "My, isn't it a beautiful little . . . Atishoo!" Algy is suddenly shaken by a violent sneeze. "Oh, do be careful. Don't drop it," cries the little bear. But he is too late. The locket has slipped from Algy's fingers.

RUPERT MEETS MRS BROWN

They greet the hedgehog with delight,
And tell him of their sorry plight.

But though they search well all around,
The precious locket can't be found.

"It's no use, Algy," Rupert sighs.
"Oh dear! Here's Mrs Brown," he cries.

She says, "There's something wrong, 'tis plain,
Please, little bear, will you explain?"

Rupert is horrified at what has happened. "Keep quite still, Algy," he cries. "The locket seemed to drop just at your feet. It must be just there." Carefully lifting the fallen oats, he searches inch by inch. "Now then, you two, what are you up to?" asks a voice. Horace the hedgehog has joined them. Rupert is delighted to see Horace. "You are just the person we need," he cries. "We've lost a gold locket just here. Do help us to find it." The hedgehog joins in cheerfully, and pushes his little nose into the grass and under the oats, but with no success.

Carefully marking the spot where the locket was dropped, the two pals wander away. As they reach the gate they see Mrs Brown bringing their lunch. "Oh, dear, I daren't face her. Let's run," cries the little pug. "That'll do no good. We must tell her," says Rupert. Mrs Brown sees there is something wrong. "Why, whatever is the matter?" she asks. "Aren't you feeling very well?" Rupert pulls himself together. "It's that locket that I was bringing to you from Mr Rabbit's shop," he says. "We've lost it!"

RUPERT GETS ADVICE

"You couldn't help it, I am sure;
Now we will go and look once more."

They have to give up for that day,
And sadly home they make their way.

"What's wrong with you?" the old man cries.
"We've lost the locket," Rupert sighs.

They leave old Jarge, and then they hear
Him call to Algy to come near.

Mrs Brown asks them to show her the exact place where the accident happened. "This was the place," says Rupert. "Well, the locket can't have run away," smiles Mrs Brown. "We'll all search for it." At length Mrs Brown says she must go. "The reaper won't be in this field until to-morrow afternoon," she says, "so there will still be time for you two to come back in the morning and have another look for the locket." The two pals move sadly homewards. As they enter Farmer Wurzel's land they notice that Gaffer Jarge is still in the field.

Gaffer Jarge stops the little friends. "Now then, what's gone wrong?" he grunts. "More mischief, I suppose." "No, not exactly," says Rupert mournfully, "but we've lost that gold locket." The old man grunts again. "That'll teach you young rascals to be more careful next time!" is all that he says. They go on into the next field while Gaffer Jarge watches them from over a gate. All at once they hear him call to Algy. The little pug runs back to him and Rupert can hear Gaffer's wheezy voice giving some sort of instructions.

RUPERT TRIES THE TURNIPS

He comes back with a puzzled air;
"What did he want?" asks Rupert Bear.

Then to the farm they run and ask,
If they may carry out their task.

To Sam the little chums explain,
And then begin to search again.

And sure enough, to their delight
The little bear has guessed aright.

Algy runs to rejoin Rupert. "What he said was rather odd," says Algy. "He told me that if the locket that we lost was not in the oats I should be sure to find it in the turnips." "Turnips?" exclaims Rupert. "But that's nonsense. All the turnips were over in the next field." Rupert tries hard to understand the meaning of the old man's words. Racing back towards Farmer Brown's land they meet Sam standing by a gate. "Hi, Sam!" cries Algy, "may we go and search for a gold locket in your turnip field?"

Sam scratches his head again as the two pals run to him. "Please, it's Mrs Brown's locket and it's Gaffer Jarge's idea," says Rupert. But this is quite beyond Sam's understanding. He just stares while the search is started. Suddenly Rupert stops searching and calls to Algy. "When you dropped the locket we thought it must be in the oats," he says, "but wise old Gaffer Jarge called you back to say it might be in your turnips . . ." But Algy doesn't wait to hear more. Feverishly he searches his left turn-up and next instant the locket is glittering in his fingers.

"We've found it, Sam," with joy they shout,
He wonders what it's all about.

To Mrs Brown they gaily bound,
To let her know the locket's found.

With lovely fruit they're loaded down,
"Please take this home," says Mrs Brown.

Says Rupert, as they ride away,
"My word! What an exciting day."

On the way to Mrs Brown they reach the field where Sam is working, and Rupert silently hands him the locket. "Well, this do beat everything!" cries the astonished farmhand. "I've worked on this farm all my life and never even found a penny. Finding gold in the turnips looks like magic to me!" Rupert and Algy laugh at the bewilderment of poor Sam. Hand-in-hand the two pals run to find Mrs Brown feeding her chickens. "Hullo," she says. "Are you going to have another look for the locket?" "No," cries Algy. "We've found it!"

The farmer's wife listens to Rupert's story with delight. Then she takes them into her orchard. "Your mothers would like a few of my apples," she smiles. "Then perhaps they won't scold you for being such a long time away from home!" Rupert and Algy decide to take turns in carrying the heavy basket, but just as they are starting, Sam appears and lifts them on to the back of his old horse, Dobbin. "This is a topping way to get home," says Rupert. "Perhaps Mr Rabbit will let me run another errand for him one of these days."

Rupert and Bill
in the
Tree Tops

A strange adventure in birdland. Telling how Uncle Bruno cured the King bird and rescued Rupert and Bill.

RUPERT AND BILL GO BLACKBERRYING

One day young Bill and Rupert go
To gather blackberries for a treat;

With picnic fare they're laden, so
They're glad to find a place to eat.

Soon after lunch they find a spot
Where blackberries very thickly grow;

But when they've gathered quite a lot
They're lost, and don't know where to go.

Bill Badger is spending his holiday with Rupert, and one day they decide to go blackberrying for Mrs Bear. Rupert takes a haversack full of sandwiches and Bill carries the ginger beer and two baskets for the fruit. They walk a long way into the country and when they reach a rocky slope Rupert stops. "I think this will be a good spot for our picnic, don't you, Bill?" he asks.

When Rupert and Bill have finished lunch, they start gathering the blackberries, and become so engrossed in their task that they wander on and on in search of the ripest fruit. After a while, when his basket is full, Rupert looks round, and is dismayed to find that he hasn't any idea in which direction they have come. "I say, Bill, do you remember the way back?" he calls, anxiously.

RUPERT ERECTS A SIGNPOST

Where three paths meet a signpost lies;
They stand it up to find the way.

"Home's through the wood," Bill gaily cries,
But Rupert's filled with much dismay.

The wood is dark, there's not a sound;
The pathway ends, and fears arise;

"We stood that signpost wrong way round,
And now we're lost, Bill," Rupert cries.

After walking a long way Rupert and Bill come to a spot where three roads meet. "Now which way do we go?" asks Bill. "Look! There is a signpost lying on the ground. Let's put it up again," says Rupert. The post is very heavy, but after a struggle the chums manage to erect it and find that the way to Nutwood lies through a dark and gloomy-looking wood.

Rupert and Bill enter the wood and follow the narrow winding path for some distance. "This doesn't seem to be leading anywhere at all," says Bill. They keep on a bit further and then the path comes to an abrupt end. Rupert suddenly realises what has happened. "We must have put the signpost up the wrong way round!" he gasps. "I hope we can find our way back," replies Bill.

RUPERT AND BILL ARE LOST

To hurry back they both agree,
But reach a stream too wide to jump;

A 'private' notice then they see;
"We're wrong," cries Bill, "I've got the hump."

The wood grows thicker all the time,
And walking gets so very slow,

They plan at length a tree to climb,
And leave the blackberries down below.

Rupert and Bill start walking through the wood, but after a few minutes they come to a wide stream. "Oh dear, we're wrong again," sighs Bill. "Cheer up," says Rupert encouragingly, "I expect we shall meet someone soon." They start off again, and then they receive another shock. "Why, these woods are private," says Rupert, pointing to a notice board on a tree.

As Rupert and Bill go further into the wood the trees become thicker and thicker until at last they find it impossible to push their way through the trunks. "There's only one thing to do," says Rupert, in desperation, "we must go up the tree." "It seems a funny idea," said Bill, doubtfully, "but I suppose we must." Leaving the baskets of blackberries on the ground they scramble up into the branches.

RUPERT MAKES A DISCOVERY

Poor Bill is feeling very sad,
So Rupert climbs up in the tree,

And soon he cries, "Such luck I've had,
Do come and see what I can see."

"Oh, isn't this a funny place!
I've found a stairway," Rupert cries.

So up the stairs they promptly race,
To where the tree-tops reach the skies.

Rupert and Bill climb about in the trees until they are very tired, and Bill collapses on a branch and begins to cry. "We shall never get out of this dreadful forest," he sighs. Rupert is determined to have one last search for a way of escape, and he climbs still higher up the tree. Suddenly Bill hears him shouting excitedly. "I wonder what he has found?" he thinks.

When Bill joins Rupert he is amazed to see a flight of steps winding through the upper branches of the trees. "This is like a fairy tale," he gasps. "Let's go up," says Rupert eagerly. After a long climb the chums reach the top and find they have pushed their way right through the trees and are out in the sunlight, with the forest rolling below them in every direction.

RUPERT AND BILL ARE ALARMED

They jump about the forest top,
Refreshed by lots of sunlit air;

Then in the sky they look, and stop—
A bird is flying towards the pair.

They run, while down the great bird flies,
And Rupert plunges through the trees,

But talons of tremendous size
Seize Bill, whose limbs with terror freeze.

Rupert and Bill step very carefully out of the hole in the trees and are amazed to find that the leaves and branches are thick enough for them to walk on. With a little practice they are able to get along quite easily and then Bill suddenly grabs Rupert's arm. "Look at that huge bird flying towards us!" he gasps in alarm.

It is clear to Rupert and Bill that the great bird has seen them and they try to run, but this is impossible on the treacherous surface of the tree tops. Rupert stumbles and falls, but the bird swoops down on Bill and clutches him in his powerful talons. Poor Bill struggles in vain as he is whirled upward, for the bird holds him in a grip of iron.

RUPERT MEETS A FRIENDLY CROW

In horror Rupert watches Bill;
"He's safe, don't worry," squawks a crow;

"To reach him, hasten on until
You find three tall trees in a row."

Now Rupert finds, beyond the trees,
A deep ravine and buildings rare;

Then on a branch a rope he sees;
"Ah, now," he says, "I'll slide down there."

Rupert gazes after Bill in dismay and is startled when a crow flies down beside him. "Don't worry," he croaks. "No harm will come to your friend." "But how can I help him?" asks Rupert. "There is one other way down from this forest," replies the crow. "Over there you will find the tops of three tall trees in line. Follow where they point!"

Rupert makes his way over the tree tops until he reaches the landmark the crow had told him to find. Following the bird's instructions, he keeps straight on, and soon comes to the edge of a deep ravine with strange buildings at the bottom. "However can I get down there?" wonders the little bear, but suddenly he catches sight of a coil of rope hanging from a branch.

RUPERT SPEAKS TO THE OWL

When Rupert lands upon the rock,
An owl explains where he must go.

Bill's captured by the Bird King's flock
Who're in the valley down below.

Below the rocky peaks he spies
The palace where, concealed, lies Bill;

But angry birds, with screeching cries,
Won't let him pass—their King is ill.

Rupert lets down the rope and climbs down to the bottom of the valley. He hurries to the first of the strange buildings and finds an owl sleepily nodding in the sunshine. "Excuse me," begins Rupert timidly, "could you please tell me where I am?" "You are in the City of the Birds," replies the owl. "That great bird has taken your friend to the palace of our King."

The owl points out the way to the palace and Rupert hurries along the valley. Rounding a corner of the rocky cliff he sees a magnificent marble building, with hundreds of birds circling round and round. Rupert starts to climb the imposing flight of steps, but is immediately surrounded by the birds, who all start screeching and crying at him at once, "The King is ill. You must not enter."

RUPERT IS TAKEN TO BILL

A lordly bird hears Rupert's tale,
And guides him to his little chum;

Cries Rupert, "Bill, aren't you in jail?"
Says Bill, "To cure the King I've come."

"Please cheer our King," implores the guide;
"Because he cannot smile he's ill."

But when their tricks and jokes they've tried
They see they've failed, he's sadder still.

Rupert pushes his way through the birds, but at the top of the steps he is stopped by an important-looking bird and to him he explains why he has come. Rupert is taken to Bill, who is delighted to see his chum and explains why he was captured. "The King never smiles now and messenger birds fly round and bring back anything they think might amuse him."

The guide takes Rupert and Bill to the King, who is looking very unhappy. "If you can amuse the King you will be rewarded," he promises. Bill tries first, and performs all kinds of tricks, but the King only looks more miserable than before. Then Rupert tells lots of funny stories, but with no more success. "I do wish we could make the King laugh," sighs Bill as they are led away.

RUPERT SENDS A MESSAGE

*Says Rupert, next day, "I've a friend
Who'll know just how to cure the King;"*

*And to the King he says, "Do send
A carrier bird my friend to bring."*

*So Rupert writes to Doctor Bear
The story of the King's distress;*

*He sees it carried through the air,
And says, "Now help is near, I guess."*

The next morning Rupert has an idea which he explains to Bill. "My Uncle Bruno is a doctor, and I am sure he could cure the King." "But do you think he would come here?" asks Bill doubtfully. Rupert writes a letter explaining what has happened, and then he asks the King if he will send his largest messenger to take the letter and bring Uncle Bruno back.

Rupert then writes out full instructions and draws a plan, so that the messenger bird will be able to find his way to Uncle Bruno's house. When all is ready the bird takes the letter and sets off on his long flight over the forest. "I do hope he will get there all right," says Rupert anxiously. "Yes," replies Bill, "and that your Uncle will not mind coming back with him."

RUPERT GREETS HIS UNCLE

They watch the skies, and soon the bird
Arrives with clever Doctor Bear,

Who to the King says, "Sir, I've heard
You need a cure from grave despair."

They gather round while Doctor Bear
Gives medicine to the monarch sad;

The King then, freed from his despair,
Begins to smile, and all feel glad.

Rupert and Bill wait on the steps for the messenger to return, and after a while they see the huge bird flying swiftly towards the palace. "Hurrah!" shouts Rupert. "Uncle Bruno has come after all." "Now we shall soon be able to go home," says Bill confidently. The courtiers look on with great interest while Dr Bear examines his patient and Rupert stands by anxiously waiting.

Amid fearful suspense, Rupert, Bill and the courtiers gather round the throne while Dr Bruno carefully measures out a spoonful of the fateful medicine and gives it to the patient. There is a long pause, and then to their great relief the King suddenly sits up Tond beams upon them. "I am cured. You have done well."

THE KING IS CURED

The King now bids his guests good-bye,
And gives to each a medal gold;

Then strong birds lift them up on high,
And take them home, as they were told.

Two birds swoop down towards Mrs Bear,
Who shrieks to Mr Bear, "Do hide!"

Then Bill and Rupert cry, "Hey, there!"
And tell their tree-top tale with pride.

Then he summons his messengers, and Rupert, Bill and Uncle Bruno say good-bye after promising to visit him some time. The powerful birds whirl them into the air and all the birds of the kingdom come to see them off. Mr and Mrs Bear are in their garden when two gigantic birds swoop down. In great fright they rush indoors and wait there until they think the coast is clear. What a happy surprise they get when they see Rupert and Bill running up the path and how amazed they are at the strange story of their adventures in the land of the tree tops.

RUPERT'S CAT SEARCH

"I always come here to Cat Corner any time I feel lonely," says Dinkie the clever kitten. "When you're lonely?" Rupert repeats in amazement. "Of course," miaows Dinkie. "There's always plenty of company here." Rupert scratches his head. "Company?" he says. "For you? I simply don't understand." "Oh dear!" Dinkie sighs. "Why do you think it's called Cat Corner?" "I've sometimes wondered about that," replies the little bear. "Why is it?" Dinkie sighs again: "Because there are so many cats here, that's why. I can see lots right now. And so could you if you'd only use your eyes!" Well, how many can *you* see?

Answer on page 117.

RUPERT'S SECRET ROUTE

"What a maze of fields and hedges there is between here and the windmill," sighs Bill Badger. Rupert laughs: "Ah, but I've found a secret route to get there. It's . . ." "No, please don't tell us!" interrupts Algy Pug. "Let Bill and I find it for ourselves." "Very well," says Rupert. "But you must remember not to go in the river and you must use only the gates and gaps in the hedges. What's more, the farmer says you mustn't go into any field with a notice board in it. Right? Then off you go!" And away scamper the other two. Algy goes over the bridge but Bill decides not to cross the water. Who finds Rupert's route?

Answer on page 117.

RUPERT

*"Just see that dark cloud over there!
It's going to pour soon, I declare!"*

One winter's day Rupert coaxes his chum Podgy Pig to go for a country walk. Although he is not keen, Podgy agrees. But he soon starts to complain and when he sees a dark cloud loom up he stops. "It's going to rain," he says, glad to find an excuse. "I knew we shouldn't have come. Let's go back." Just then the rain begins and as large drops patter down, Rupert calls out: "There's a barn. Let's run for it!"

and the FLAVOURS

"Let's shelter!" Rupert tells his chum
Who cries, "I wish we hadn't come!"

Rupert dashes ahead and gets to the barn first. "Oh, what a downpour!" he pants. "Still, I don't think it will last . . ." He swings round to find that Podgy is no longer with him. Then to his dismay he sees his chum lying on his back in the rain with his mouth wide open. "Oh, he must have hurt himself," Rupert thinks and, throwing an old piece of sacking over his shoulders for protection from the rain, he runs to help Podgy.

Mouth open, Podgy lies down flat.
Gasps Rupert, "What's he playing at?"

"Is Podgy hurt?" He dons a sack
To keep him dry then hurries back.

RUPERT MEETS THE INVENTOR

Says Podgy as he smacks his lips,
"This rain tastes just like fish and chips!"

"You can't lie here! You're getting wet!
We'll dash for shelter. Up you get!"

"That rain was flavoured like I said.
Try some." But Rupert shakes his head.

A voice, when it is fine again,
Asks, "What did you think of the rain?"

"Podgy! Are you hurt?" Rupert asks anxiously as he reaches his chum. But the little pig sits up and says brightly, "Of course not. I was having a drink of this lovely rain. It tastes just like fish and chips!" Rupert looks hard at Podgy and says, "Come on, stop fooling. You'll be soaked if you stay out here." Podgy starts to say, "I mean it . . ." but Rupert pulls him to his feet and, covering his shoulders with the sacking, leads him to the barn. Once the pals are under cover Podgy says, "It's

true. The rain really does taste like fish and chips. Try it yourself." But before Rupert can answer, the rain stops and at almost the same moment a voice behind them says, "Well, my little friends, what did you think of the rain, eh?" And the chums turn to find the tall, quiet man they know as the Inventor. "I've been keeping an eye on you," he smiles. Rupert wonders what the man meant about the rain, particularly just after what Podgy has said about it.

86

RUPERT TASTES THE RAIN

"*What Podgy told you was no lie
The rain is tasty. Have a try!*"

So Rupert tries a few small sips.
"*You're right! It tastes of fish and chips!*"

"*Yes, I can make rain taste of fish
Or any other food I wish.*"

"*Ice cream and toffee apples, too,
Just right for plumpish folk like you.*"

"I came out to catch a sample of the rain," the Inventor explains. "I designed this just for the job," he adds, showing the pals the odd umbrella he is carrying. They can see that he has indeed collected rainwater in the upturned brim. "When I saw one of you lying in the rain with his mouth open I guessed the flavour had been discovered. You, little bear, didn't believe your friend so you'd both better try it." And he holds the odd umbrella low so that the two pals can dip their fingers in the water and taste it. "Why, it does taste just like fish and chips!" exclaims Rupert. "But how?" The Inventor chuckles quietly. "I put the flavour into the rain," he says. "Indeed, I can make the rain any flavour I choose. It's my latest idea." "Even ice-cream and toffees?" asks Podgy with shining eyes. "Anything at all," says the Inventor. "It's just the thing for plump folk like you." And he prods Podgy. "Now if you will come with me I'll see how much you weigh."

RUPERT IS ASKED TO HELP

"My rain, instead of too much food,
Would keep folk slim and still taste good."

"I shan't weigh Rupert since he's slim.
I have a special job for him."

"I pump up flavours which are sprayed
On rainclouds from this mast I've made."

"Empty the brolly, please, with care,
While I weigh Podgy, little bear."

On the way the Inventor tells the chums about his plans. "If only people would drink my tasty rainwater instead of eating so much," he declares, "they'd stay slim." "Will you want to weigh both of us?" asks Rupert. The Inventor gives him the umbrella to carry. "No," he replies. "Only your friend. You're slim enough. But there is one thing you can do for me. I've heard that you are good at climbing." Just then they arrive at the Inventor's house. Beside it stands a girder mast stretching up to the sky. "This mast," says the Inventor, "has a sprinkler at the top. I pump up whichever flavour I choose and spray it on to the rain clouds. The liquid comes from this big tank here." Then telling Rupert to empty the umbrella into a bucket, he leads Podgy off to be weighed. As he empties the umbrella Rupert wonders what sort of job the Inventor has for him. "He said it had something to do with climbing," muses the little bear. "What could it be?"

RUPERT IS TOLD HIS TASK

The speak-your-weight machine's voice shakes,
"T-twenty tons . . . crrrang !" Then breaks!

"You're far too heavy, that's well seen!
You've ruined my brand new machine!"

"I've tried to climb the mast but felt
Too dizzy. Use this safety belt."

"For you must climb the mast and seek
The spot that drips and seal the leak."

Rupert empties the sample of rainwater into the bucket and carries it into the house in time to see Podgy step on to a weighing machine. "Keep perfectly still," the Inventor is saying, "and it will speak your weight. It switches itself on." There is a click then a spluttering voice comes from a loudspeaker. "T-twenty tons . . . sptzz! . . . burr! . . . ping! . . . five grammes . . . eighty pounds . . . crrrang!" The Inventor drags Podgy off the machine. "You're so heavy you've damaged it!" he exclaims. The Inventor strides around the room looking cross. "It is most upsetting when things go wrong!" Then he stops and peers at Rupert. "Ah yes! That climbing job!" He opens a big box and takes out a belt with a chain attached. "Put this on for safety. You'll be going very high." The little bear is puzzled. "But where am I going?" he asks. "Why, up the mast to find a leak in the flavours pipe and mend it," the Inventor replies. "I'd go, but heights make me dizzy."

RUPERT'S PAL MAKES A MISTAKE

Some tubes marked "Flavours" Podgy spies,
And samples one. "Yumm-yumm!" he cries.

"Stop! Stop! One sip is flavour for
Five hundred puddings—even more!"

"You'll have to take this antidote!"
A dose is poured down Podgy's throat.

"Now, little bear, it's starting time.
A thousand feet you'll have to climb!"

"I am quite sure the leak is near the top of the mast," the Inventor explains to Rupert. "And it must be sealed as soon as possible." While he is talking Podgy wanders off into the next room. He spots a row of tubes marked "Flavours". What a chance to try them, he thinks, and putting one to his mouth, takes a swig. "Yumm! Scrumptious!" he murmurs. Just then the Inventor sees what Podgy is up to and darts in to snatch the tube from him. "Foolish thing!" he shouts. "That is extra strong essence. One sip is equal to five hundred whole chocolate puddings!" Hurriedly he produces a big bottle and makes Podgy take a spoonful from it. "This will take away the effect," he says. And though Podgy shudders and squirms, he has to take several doses. By the time the Inventor leads Rupert out to the mast Podgy is feeling very sorry for himself. Rupert peers up the tall mast. "How high must I climb?" he asks. "A thousand feet," is the reply.

RUPERT CLIMBS THE MAST

Poor Rupert pleads, with quaking knees,
"Oh, couldn't someone else go, please?"

Making sure the chain is fast,
Rupert starts to scale the mast.

"So high, and still can't see the top!
Ah, there's the leak that I must stop."

"Make sure that this repair patch sticks.
I hope that it's not hard to fix."

The thought of having to climb so high fills the little bear with alarm. A thousand feet! "Isn't there anyone else who could do this for you?" he asks, pausing on the ladder. "But of course not," replies the Inventor irritably. "I wouldn't ask you otherwise. You don't expect your plump chum to go up, do you?" Plucking up his courage and taking a deep breath, Rupert starts to climb the mast, hooking the safety chain above him every few rungs. After a while he stops and looks at the ground far below. "I don't like this at all," he thinks. The climb seems endless and he can't see the top of the mast which is hidden in the clouds. Then he spots a small hole in the pipe beside the mast. "That must be the leak the Inventor spoke of," he thinks. He takes the repair patch from the pouch the Inventor has given him and examines the hole. To reach it he has to lean right out at the end of the safety chain. "If . . . if I should fall now . . ." he thinks with a shudder.

"I've reached the flavour-sprinkler! Whew!
A bird is perching on it, too!"

The bird caws loudly, "You down there,
Explain this monstrous thing, young bear!"

"Flavour the rain! Our pure supply
Of drinking water! Let him try!"

"You warn that foolish flavours man,
We'll take revenge and foil his plan!"

Taking care not to look down, Rupert soon fixes the sticky patch over the hole in the pipe then takes a firm hold on the ladder again. Suddenly the clouds part and he sees that he is near the top of the high mast. "That tube at the top with holes in it must be the Inventor's sprinkler for spraying the clouds with flavours. I say, there's a big bird perched on it!" Just then the bird spots Rupert. "Come up here, little bear!" it caws loudly. Carefully Rupert makes his way to the top. "What

is the meaning of this thing?" demands the bird. Clinging to the mast, Rupert tries to explain to the bird about the Inventor's ideas. "How dare he!" squawks the bird. "All we Nutwood birds depend on the rain for our drinking water. We don't want his horrid flavours." It wheels angrily round the mast then returns and cries: "Warn the man that unless he stops spoiling the rain we birds will take our revenge." And with that it flies off towards the distant woods.

RUPERT PASSES ON A WARNING

Now Rupert's anxious to descend
And take the warning to his friend.

"Bah! Those birds protest in vain!
They'll soon get used to flavoured rain."

"More rain forecast. No time to lose!
Which flavour would you like to choose?"

And as the chums head home again
Podgy gloats about fruity rain.

Rupert is keener than ever to get back to the ground again. But the journey down the mast is slow for he has to fasten and unfasten his safety chain every few steps. At length he reaches the bottom to be met by the Inventor and Podgy. He tells the man that he has repaired the pipe then goes on to repeat the bird's warning. But the Inventor is scornful. "Bah! What can birds do?" he scoffs. "My plan is far too important to be stopped now. They'll get used to the flavours in time." He stalks back to his house followed by the pals. "I must be ready for the next spell of rain," he mutters, studying a barometer. "I see it's becoming colder and we shall have more rain. I must prepare another flavour. What shall it be this time, eh?" "Oh, please, fruit salad!" Podgy pleads. "Good idea," muses the Inventor. "Fruit salad it shall be." On the way home the little pig talks about nothing else. "Well, just don't lie in it this time!" laughs Rupert.

RUPERT HELPS PODGY'S PLAN

"Mummy's been cooking—what a spread!
Still, I'll wait for that rain instead."

"I tried a Flavour and somehow
I'm not the least bit hungry now."

"Help me," pleads Podgy, then the chums
Fetch bowls for when the rainfall comes.

"Spread all of them across this plot
Then I shall catch a lovely lot!"

When the pals reach Podgy's home the little pig invites Rupert to stay a while. "Mummy's been cooking," whispers Podgy, gazing at the goodies spread out on the table. "It's just a snack for you, Podgy," smiles Mrs Pig. But the little pig won't touch a morsel. "I tasted some stuff at the Inventor's house," he explains, "and I'm not very hungry now." "Yes, it was all part of an idea for flavouring rain," chimes in Rupert. And the pals start to describe their adventure, but Mrs Pig soon gives up trying to make any sense of it. "I can't spare any more time," she declares. As she returns to her work, Podgy collects as many big bowls as he can find. "Come on, Rupert, give me a hand," he asks. "I'm going to set these out to collect that fruit salad rain when it comes. I shall have a wonderful time!" And although Rupert smiles and shakes his head at Podgy's greediness, he joins in and together they begin to spread the bowls all over the lawn.

RUPERT TELLS HIS DADDY

"Hi, Daddy!" Rupert gives a yell.
"I have the strangest thing to tell!"

"That puddle's flavoured too, you'll find!"
"What! I'll do nothing of the kind!"

"Brr-rr! It's freezing!" Mummy says
And stirs the fire into a blaze.

"Rupert, wake up! The world's all white!
We've had a snowfall in the night."

After helping Podgy, Rupert sets off for home. On the way he sees his Daddy just ahead of him. "Hullo, Daddy, you'll never guess the adventure I've had!" he cries. And as they stroll along he tells Mr Bear everything that has taken place at the Inventor's house. But Mr Bear treats it as just another of Rupert's rambling tales. "Rain that tastes of fish and chips! You're pulling my leg!" he says. "Truly I'm not," insists the little bear. "Even that puddle over there on the road is flavoured."

"I don't think I'll taste it anyway," grins Daddy. Later that evening Mrs Bear stirs the fire to a blaze. "It's turning really cold," she says. "Perhaps we shall have snow." At the word "snow" Rupert looks up from his book. He remembers the Inventor's plans and wonders if the snow will be flavoured too. Then he thinks, "Perhaps it won't really snow." But next morning Daddy wakes him early. "Look! We've had a heavy fall of snow," he announces.

95

"You're right! This snow does have a taste!"
Then Rupert cries, "No time to waste!"

"It's frozen—ponds and rivers too!
Whatever will the poor birds do?"

"I'd better find those birds. I think
They won't like flavoured snow to drink,"

"Fruit-flavoured snowballs do taste nice!
Much better than vanilla ice."

Snow! At once Rupert is wide awake. His Daddy scoops a handful of snow off the windowsill. "Up you get!" he laughs. "Now you really will be able to have some fun!" As he turns to go Rupert asks, "Does that snow in your hand have any taste?" Mr Bear repeats, "Taste?" But he puts it to his lips and tries. "Yes, it has!" he exclaims, amazed. "Like . . . fruit salad!" And he recalls Rupert's adventure of the day before. Later in the garden they find the bird bath is frozen solid. "All the streams and ponds will be frozen too," Rupert says worriedly. "What will the birds do?" Then still worrying he sets out to find some of the Nutwood birds. "They peck snow when there's no drinking water," he thinks, "but they will hate the taste of this flavoured stuff!" Just then he meets his pal with an armful of snowballs. "Can't stop to play, Podgy," Rupert begins. But Podgy grunts and says, "Don't want to play. I've made these snowballs to eat. They taste just like fruit salad!"

But Rupert presses quickly on.
"One bird! Where have the others gone?"

"Too thirsty now to fly or sing,
They've gathered by our secret spring."

"Come, follow me," the bird cries. "Please!"
And leads the way into the trees.

"Our secret pool is frozen thick.
We cannot break it. Help us, quick!"

Leaving Podgy to gloat over his flavoured snow-balls, Rupert presses on towards the woods. There is a strange hush everywhere as he plods through the snow, and the birds are not in their usual haunts. At last Rupert sees one hunched miserably on a branch. "Where are all your friends?" asks Rupert anxiously. "I've come to see if you need drinking water." "Yes, we do," replies the bird. "When times are hard we rely on our secret spring of water. But now we can't even drink from that."

Rupert looks so dismayed that the bird says, "See for yourself if you like. I'll show you the way." With an effort the bird rises and flutters ahead of Rupert. "Keep in sight," it calls. And soon Rupert is being led through parts of the wood he has never seen before. At last they reach a tiny pool hidden among rocks. Unhappy looking birds are gathered round the frozen water. "This is our secret spring," says Rupert's guide. "But the ice is so thick we can't break it."

RUPERT CANNOT BREAK THE ICE

"With snow we cannot quench our thirst.
This horrid flavour's quite the worst!"

He hits the ice with might and main,
But Rupert's efforts are in vain.

"How can we wait until the thaw?
It's that man's fault!" the poor birds caw.

"We'll make him sorry! What a waste
To give pure rain that nasty taste!"

At first the birds are wary of Rupert, but when they learn that he has come to try to help them they all cluster around him, chattering at once. "We've had nothing to drink since the icy weather began," chirps one. "And we can't peck the snow because it tastes so horrid," pipes another. "And now our spring of pure water is frozen solid," a blackbird adds. "Perhaps I can break the ice on your spring," suggests Rupert. But although he hammers the ice hard with a piece of rock it is too solid for him. "It's no use, I'm afraid," he pants. "I can't crack it." There is an angry sort of murmuring among the birds around the pool. "It is all the fault of that man," one of them chirps. "Our scout found he was sprinkling stuff on the clouds to give the rain the kind of flavours that people like." "Yes," agrees Rupert. "First fish and chips. Now fruit salad." Suddenly the birds begin to swarm around Rupert. "Revenge!" they cry angrily. "We'll make that man sorry! Revenge!"

RUPERT WARNS THE INVENTOR

The birds take off in vengeful crowds
And fill the sky like angry clouds.

"This snow experiment's my best.
And now to do a flavour test."

"The birds are angry! Please take care!"
Blurts out the anxious little bear.

Now birds crowd on the window sill,
Angry, screeching, wild and shrill!

The birds sweep past Rupert and soar above the trees, still screeching their anger. "I wonder what they mean to do," Rupert worries. "Maybe I'd better let the Inventor know." Retracing his own footprints in the snow, Rupert makes his way out of the wood. As he hurries towards the house of the Inventor the sky is streaked with clouds of birds gathering from all quarters. Rupert finds the Inventor filling a pail with snow. "Hello," he says. "I wasn't expecting you. I'm taking this snow in to test its flavour . . ." "Please!" Rupert interrupts. "The birds are terribly angry because you flavoured the rain. Hundreds of them are coming here for their revenge!" "Rubbish!" snorts the Inventor. "They can't harm me. You're making a fuss over nothing. Now come and watch me test this snow." But Rupert is very uneasy as he follows the Inventor indoors. When they reach the workroom birds are already starting to flutter against the windows.

RUPERT PLEADS WITH THE BIRDS

The window's dark with screaming birds.
The noise! Too terrible for words!

"Stop! I give in! I'll end my tests.
Please make them go back to their nests!"

Rupert runs out to tell the crowd
Of birds, "You've won! Don't screech so loud!"

"He says he wants you all to know
No more he'll flavour rain or snow!"

Even as Rupert and the Inventor watch, the birds grow in numbers until the windows are darkened by them. The noise of their angry screeching fills the room. "Oh, I can't stand this!" the Inventor cries. "It's terrible. Stop! Stop!" But still the noise goes on and on until at last, looking pale and frightened, the Inventor turns to Rupert. "I give in!" he shouts above the uproar. "Make them stop and I'll promise never to experiment with rain again!"

"I'll tell them at once!" cries Rupert and he dashes outside and scrambles up the stairs that lead to the flat roof. When the birds see him they swarm up from the windows, circling angrily. Rupert waves his arms and calls loudly, "Birds! You've won!" The birds stop wheeling in order to hear Rupert. "You've won!" he repeats. "The Inventor begs you to stop. He says that if you leave him in peace he promises never to put any sort of stuff in the rain again!"

RUPERT ASKS FOR MEDICINE

"I think they're waiting, every bird,
To make sure that you keep your word."

Now the Inventor, moving fast,
Makes straight towards the giant mast.

"We'll add this liquid to make sure
The snow that's due is once more pure."

"Save me a little of that stuff,"
Begs Rupert, "when you've used enough."

Now the birds are all silent. But they watch Rupert as he makes his way back to the Inventor. The little bear hopes that they have understood his message. Inside the workroom again he tells the Inventor, "I think they understand and that they are waiting to see what you'll do." "Yes, I must show them that I intend to keep my promise," says the man. "I couldn't stand any more noise." Then he picks up a bottle. It is the one he used to dose Podgy when the little pig drank the strong essence.

"I'll put this in the sprinkler. It'll take away the flavour of the snow." Carefully he pours the stuff from the bottle into the tank as the birds watch in silence. "I can't sprinkle it until the next fall of snow," he adds. "But there is more due very soon." Suddenly Rupert remembers something. "Can you save a little of that stuff?" he asks. "I shall need it later." "Of course," says the surprised Inventor. "You may have what is left now. But why do you want it?"

RUPERT'S PAL FEELS UNWELL

"Podgy may need another dose,"
He tells the man and off he goes.

The bird squawks, "He means well, we think.
But just the same, what can we drink?"

"Fruit salad snowballs!" Podgy moans.
"They've given me tummy-ache!" he groans.

"Come on!" says Rupert. "Get this down!
Oh, yes, you must! No use to frown."

Rupert points towards the village. "On the way here I met my friend Podgy," he explains. "He was about to have a feast of flavoured snowballs and I'm afraid he might make himself ill. So I need some of this stuff, just in case." The Inventor nods. "Most thoughtful of you," he says. "And if you get the chance tell the birds that the next fall of snow will dissolve the flavour of the last fall." So Rupert sets off with the bottle and he has not gone far when some birds swoop down beside him. When they hear what he has to say one of them cheeps, "That's all very well but what do we drink in the meantime?" Rupert is still trying to think of an answer when he spies Podgy propped up against a tree. "Oooo! I've such a tummy-ache," he wails. "I ate too many of those fruit salad snowballs." "I thought so," says Rupert. "Lucky for you the Inventor gave me what was left of this stuff." "Oh, not that again!" begs Podgy. But Rupert makes him drink it.

RUPERT GETS A CALLER

The special cure works like a charm
And Podgy's led away from harm.

"You leave those snowballs where they are!
Now, home we go! It isn't far!"

Now Rupert's Mummy hears him tell
How with the snow all will be well.

A scrumptious meal awaits the pair.
Then comes a knock! "I'll see who's there!"

Although Podgy splutters and complains all the time Rupert is making him swallow the Inventor's cure, he is soon feeling well again. "Good, then let's go home," says Rupert. Even now Podgy can't resist a glance back at the snowballs he has left behind. "Seems such a waste . . ." he begins, but Rupert takes hold of his arm. "No, you are not going back for them. You'd only make yourself ill again!" And still holding Podgy's arm firmly, he marches him homewards.

At home Rupert has lots to tell his Mummy, but his story leaves her quite bewildered. "So, you see, everything will be put right with the next fall of snow," he ends. "Well, that's amazing!" gasps Mrs Bear. "But don't leave Podgy out there, Rupert. Ask him in for lunch." The little pig's appetite has returned and as he starts on a large bowl of soup he chuckles, "Real food's best after all." Just then there is a knock at the front door. "I'll go, Mummy," Rupert says.

RUPERT MELTS THE ICE

It's the Inventor come to bring
Some powder. "Now the birds can sing!"

"A little powder on the ice
Will melt the thickest in a trice."

One pinch, and where the ice has been,
Pure water, crystal clear, is seen.

The first bird drinks and starts to sing.
"Next," laugh the chums, "the secret spring!"

Rupert opens the door to find the Inventor. "I have called to give you this," he says and hands Rupert a small box. "After you'd gone I recalled a powder I once invented for turning ice back into water. This is it and I thought you'd like it to keep the birds happy until the snow comes." "Oh, thank you!" exclaims Rupert. "It's just what they need!" Podgy joins him in time to see the man at the gate and to hear him call, "Just sprinkle a little on the ice. It works very quickly."

As soon as Rupert and Podgy have finished their lunch they hurry out to the bird-bath which is still frozen hard. "This will make a good test," Rupert says, sprinkling some of the powder on the ice. In just a few moments the ice melts. "The birds will be so happy!" laughs Podgy. "Yes, and this afternoon I'm going to use it on the bird's secret spring in the woods," says Rupert. "Come on let's both go. We can tell them this is the Inventor's way of saying he's sorry."

MAKE A
CHRISTMAS TREE
JUST LIKE RUPERT'S

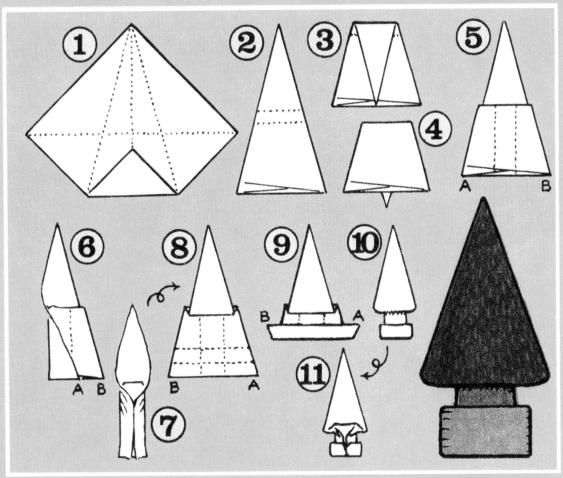

You will need a square of thin paper. Fold opposite corners together each way to find the middle and fold one corner part way to the centre (Fig. 1). Fold both sides in along the sloping dotted lines (Fig. 2), note the new dotted lines and bring the top point to the middle of the bottom edge to give the upper crease (Fig. 3) and then fold the point backwards using the other dotted line (Fig 4). Bring the point up again keeping both folds pressed (Fig. 5) and mark two upright lines, as shown, at equal distances from the corners A and B. Take A across to a spot on the bottom edge that will make a fold at the lefthand dotted line. Press that fold only as far up as the middle crease (Fig. 6) and do the same to B so that A and B can be held forward together (Fig. 7). Separate A and B as in Fig. 5 and turn the paper over (Fig. 8). Fold the bottom edge up, then over again, following the horizontal dotted lines (Fig. 9). Take B and A round to the back and the creases of Figs. 6 and 7 will cause the Christmas tree (Fig. 10) to take shape. Turn it over again (Fig. 11), lock the end of B into A, then gently flatten the folds at the back into the form required. If the 'tub' is slightly rounded the tree will stand up.

(This version of his Christmas tree was sent to Rupert by Mr Robert Harbin, the Origami man.)

RUPERT and the

"Hello!" calls Rupert eagerly.
"We're off to buy a Christmas tree!"

It is a snowy December morning and Rupert and Mr Bear are on their way to buy a Christmas tree. As they walk along the High Street, Rupert spots some of his chums, peering in the window of the toy shop. "Hello!" calls Bill. "Not long to wait for Christmas now!" When they reach the greengrocer's Mr Bear stops with a gasp. "Dear me!" he cries. "They haven't got a single tree left! Let's go in and see what's wrong . . ."

Christmas Tree

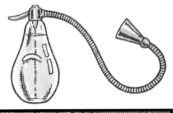

But when they reach the shop, the pair
Soon learn that there are no trees there!

"I'm sorry! They're in short supply.
The forest's sick. I don't know why!"

"Sorry!" says Mr Chimp. "I normally order lots of trees for Christmas, but this year there just aren't any to be found. Something's wrong with the forest and none of the pine or spruce are good enough to use!" "What a shame!" says Rupert. "It won't be the same without a tree . . ." As the pair leave the shop someone else is reading the dismal sign. "Bodkin!" says Rupert. "He must have come to buy a tree for the Professor . . ."

Outside the grocer's Rupert sees
Bodkin reading about the trees . . .

RUPERT SHARES A PROBLEM

"None left!" he gasps. "But I've been sent.
For one for an experiment . . ."

"I'd better go and see what's wrong.
Perhaps you'd like to come along?"

"One tree's enough!" calls Mr Bear.
"We'll put it in the village square!"

The old Professor's shocked to find
He can't buy trees of any kind!

"No trees!" cries the Professor's servant. "I don't believe it . . ." When he hears what's wrong, Bodkin explains that his master needs a Christmas tree for his latest experiment. "He's invented a potion to stop the needles falling off. If I can't find a tree, then how will we ever know if it works?" Thinking for a moment, he tells Rupert he plans to go to the forest to see what's wrong. "Why don't you come too?" he asks. "If we find a healthy tree you can help me carry it back."

Mr Bear thinks that going to the forest for a tree is a good idea. "Good luck!" he calls as the pair set out. "If you find a nice one we can put it in the village square . . ." Following Bodkin across the snowy fields, Rupert hurries towards the Professor's tower. "Hello!" blinks his old friend. "This *is* a pleasant surprise! But where's the tree I wanted?" "There aren't any!" shrugs Bodkin. "Goodness!" gasps the Professor. "How odd! Come in and tell me what's happened . . ."

"I've made a tonic that should stop
Trees letting all their needles drop!"

"Come on!" calls Bodkin. "Off we go!
I'll tow you there, across the snow . . ."

Beyond the common, Rupert sees
A forest full of tall pine trees.

The pines grow side by side, packed tight,
So dense there's hardly any light.

Leading the way to his laboratory, the Professor shows Rupert the new potion. "It's a special tree tonic!" he explains. "Falling needles should be a thing of the past, although I need to try it out on a Christmas tree before I can be certain!" "Bodkin and I are going into the woods to look for one!" says Rupert excitedly. "He said we'd use a sledge to carry it back . . ." When everything is ready, Bodkin tells Rupert to climb aboard. "Hold tight!" he calls. "We're on our way!"

Swishing across the common, Rupert soon spots the beginning of Nutwood forest. Even the familiar trees look different under a heavy blanket of snow. On the far side of the wood, the pair come to a steep hill, which they whizz down together, with Bodkin riding on the back of the sledge. When their ride ends, they find themselves at the edge of the pine forest. The trees here are tall and close together, while the way ahead looks dark and gloomy . . .

RUPERT MEETS THE PINE KING

"This tree looks perfect! Not too big,"
Says Bodkin and prepares to dig . . .

Green spiky woodland Imps appear.
"Our King has banned all digging here!"

The Pine King comes. "What's this I see?
I cannot spare a single tree!"

"The pines are sick! Their needles fall.
Some unknown blight has struck them all!"

Following a narrow track through the trees, Rupert and Bodkin make their way into the silent forest. The tall pines are much too big to take back to Nutwood, but in a clearing they come across a smaller tree that looks ideal. "Perfect!" says Bodkin. "As soon as I've dug it up, you can help me load it aboard." He is about to begin, when the silence of the forest is broken by an angry cry. "Stop!" calls a shrill voice. "The Pine King has forbidden the taking of trees . . ."

To Rupert and Bodkin's astonishment, they find themselves surrounded by an angry group of woodland Imps . . . "We didn't mean any harm," begins Rupert, then breaks off as he spots an imposing figure, wearing a crown of cones. "What's this?" demands the King. "Who dares disturb the silence of Our Realm?" When he hears what Rupert and Bodkin want, he tells them a terrible blight has struck the forest. "The trees are all sickly and shedding their needles!"

"We'd like to save the forest too . . .
If only I knew what to do!"

Then Rupert smiles. "There is a way!
Let's hurry back without delay . . ."

"The old Professor holds the key.
His tonic sounds just right to me!"

The pair explain what's wrong, and how
They hope to save the pine trees now.

"So that's why there are no Christmas trees this year!" gasps Rupert. "Aye!" declares the Pine King. "My guards have strict orders. Until the forest recovers, there can be no trees to spare!" "But that's terrible!" says Rupert. "If only there was something we could do . . ." Then he suddenly has a good idea. "Perhaps we *can* help save the forest after all!" he tells the King. "Come on, Bodkin. Follow me! We've got to get back to Nutwood as quickly as we can . . ."

As they set out for Nutwood, Rupert tells Bodkin what he has in mind. "The Professor's new tonic!" he smiles. "If it can stop trees shedding their needles, then perhaps it can make them better too?" The pair speed back on the sledge, then run breathlessly into the tower to tell the Professor everything that has happened. "Dear me!" he cries. "I had no idea the forest was in such a sorry state. I don't know if my mixture will do the trick, but it's certainly worth a try . . ."

RUPERT TELLS THE PROFESSOR

"It might help," Rupert's friend agrees.
'We'll spray it on the weakest trees . . ."

"I'll fly above the trees. Your task
Will be to spray them from this flask."

"We need to hover very low
And spray the forest as we go."

They fly to where the pine wood lies.
"Get ready!" the Professor cries.

"We'll have to spray the trees from above!" declares the Professor. "Bodkin can get a flying machine ready, while you help in the laboratory." "Can I fly in the plane too?" asks Rupert. "Of course!" smiles his friend. "You and Bodkin can work the spray together." The Professor pours all the tonic into a large flask, then fixes a long hose to the top. "We haven't got enough to cover the whole forest," he tells Rupert, "so your job is to pick out the most needy-looking trees . . ."

When Rupert and the Professor go outside, they find that Bodkin has already wheeled the flying machine from its hangar. "I'll start the engine!" calls the Professor. "You and Rupert climb aboard and we'll be on our way . . ." In no time at all, the friends are soaring high above the snow-covered fields of Nutwood and on towards the Pine King's forest. "We'll try to hover just above the tree-tops," explains the Professor. "Don't start spraying until I've got as close as I can . . ."

RUPERT SPRAYS THE TREES

"Start now!" he calls out. "Fire away!"
So Rupert starts to aim the spray.

"That's it!" cries Rupert. "One tree done!
Now I'll begin another one . . ."

At last the flask is empty, then
The three fly homeward once again.

"But will it work?" "We'll have to wait!
You'd better go now. Don't be late!"

Circling over the blighted pine forest, the Professor's plane sinks lower and lower, until it is just above the tops of the trees. Steadying the heavy flask, Bodkin starts to pump the handle, while Rupert takes aim with the spray. "Now!" calls the Professor. Bodkin turns a lever and a fine mist drenches the nearest tree. Moving forward, they spray the next pine, then another and another, until Rupert loses count. "Well done!" cries the Professor. "Excellent work!"

Spraying the pine trees takes a long time and it is late afternoon before Rupert's work is done. "We've used every last drop of tonic!" declares Bodkin as his master flies back to Nutwood. "I wonder if the Pine King saw us?" By the time they land, the sky is growing dark and Rupert has to hurry home for tea. "Do you think the trees will get better now?" he asks the Professor. "I hope so," smiles his friend, "but I don't really know. All we can do is wait until tomorrow . . ."

RUPERT'S PLAN WORKS

Next morning, Rupert wakes to find
The presents Santa's left behind . . .

Then Bodkin calls. "I'm off to see
The pine trees. Will you come with me?"

"I hope the tonic's done the trick!
The poorly pines might still be sick . . ."

"Look!" Bodkin cries. "They're thick and green!
The healthiest I've ever seen!"

Next morning, Rupert wakes up to find a bulging stocking at the foot of his bed. "Christmas Day!" he cries and peers inside to see what presents Santa has left. After breakfast, there is a knock at the door and Bodkin wishes everyone a happy Christmas. "I've come to ask if Rupert would like to go to the forest," he explains. "We can see if the Professor's tonic has made any difference to the sickly trees . . ." "Good idea!" smiles Mrs Bear. "But don't be late for Christmas dinner!"

Striding out across the snow-covered common, Bodkin warns Rupert that the Professor isn't sure his tonic will have done the trick. "He only made it for indoor trees," he says. "Pines in a forest might not like it at all . . ." As they reach the edge of the wood he breaks off with a startled cry. "Look at the difference!" he gasps. The pine trees are greener and bushier than Rupert has ever seen them and even the smallest saplings seem to have grown taller. "Wonderful!" he cries.

RUPERT IS REWARDED

Then, one by one, Pine Imps appear.
"Your magic spray has worked!" they cheer.

The King arrives. "You've saved my trees!
There's no trace left of their disease!"

Now that the King has trees to spare,
He gives one to the helpful pair.

The Imps have a surprise planned too.
"We'll carry the tree back for you!"

As Rupert and Bodkin stand admiring the trees, they hear a rustling sound nearby. One by one the Pine King's subjects appear, dancing with delight at how the forest has recovered. "Hurray!" calls their leader. "The Pine Wood has been saved, all thanks to you!" "Bravo!" booms a deep voice as the King himself comes to thank Rupert and Bodkin. "We saw you flying over the forest yesterday," he marvels. "Your spray has worked wonders! The pines have never looked so healthy and green! Now that the forest has recovered, there are plenty of trees to spare," smiles the King. "As a sign of our gratitude, we have chosen one specially for the village of Nutwood!" As he speaks, more Pine Imps appear, carrying a splendid tree. "Hurrah!" cries Rupert. "We *will* have a Christmas tree, after all!" Bidding farewell to the King, Rupert and Bodkin set off home, with the little Imps carrying the tree behind them. "What a sight!" chuckles Bodkin.

Rupert and the Christmas Tree

RUPERT'S PALS JOIN IN

When Nutwood comes in sight, they go.
"We can't let people see, you know!"

Soon Rupert's chums all run to see
The wonderful new Christmas tree.

They all bring decorations, and
Soon have a special party planned . . .

That evening, everybody comes.
"A fine tree!" Gaffer tells the chums.

When they reach the outskirts of Nutwood, the Pine Imps tell Rupert they dare not come any further for fear of being seen. "Never mind!" he smiles. "I'm sure Bodkin and I can manage from here. Thanks again for such a splendid gift!" Hauling the tree through the snow, the pair soon spot some of Rupert's chums, who come running to help . . . "What a marvellous tree!" gasps Willie. "We're going to put it in the village square," explains Rupert. "Wonderful!" calls Algy.

As soon as the villagers hear about the Christmas tree, they all offer to help decorate it straightaway. "Splendid!" beams the Professor as Bodkin clambers up a ladder. "I think our little tree-spraying experiment was a definite success . . ." Later that evening, as darkness falls, everyone gathers round the tree to sing carols and wish each other Happy Christmas. "Well done!" Gaffer Jarge tells Rupert. "'Tis the finest tree I've ever seen!"

Follow
RUPERT
every morning in the
DAILY EXPRESS

ANSWERS TO THE PUZZLES
Page 82. There are eighteen cats besides Dinkie.
Page 83. Algy finds the way.